# CANEBRAKE BEACH

# Canebrake Beach

## A Novella and Four Stories

JOHN M. KEITH

NEWSOUTH BOOKS
Montgomery

NewSouth Books
105 S. Court Street
Montgomery, AL 36104

ISBN-13: 978-1-60306-231-2 (paperback)
ISBN-10: 1-60306-231-9 (paperback)
ISBN-13: 978-1-60306-232-9 (ebook)
ISBN-10: 1-60306-232-7 (ebook)

Printed in the United States of America

TO

MY SISTER, ANN KEITH CRONAN,

AND MY BROTHER, THOMAS LATIMER KEITH,

WHO SHARE CHILDHOOD MEMORIES

OF OUR FARM IN GEORGIA

# Contents

# Canebrake Beach

*When I was a child, I spoke like a child,*
*I thought like a child, I reasoned like a child;*
*when I became a man, I gave up childish ways.*
*For now we see in a mirror dimly,*
*but then face to face.*
*Now I know in part; then I shall understand fully,*
*Even as I have been full understood*

St. Paul, I Corinthians 13: 11–12
(Revised Standard Version)

## SUMMER OF 1945

On a hot July afternoon Byron Ashford stepped out of his mother's car in front of the Mosses' house. Irene Ashford changed gears with a lever on the floor of the black Plymouth her husband had bought several years before the war. It was the first time that Byron had been left by himself with the Mosses, the white tenant family that had lived on the Ashford farm for over two decades. Usually his mother sent word for DeLane to come up to the big house to play with him when she went into town for a women's missionary meeting at the Presbyterian Church.

Byron came down to the Mosses' house two or three times almost every week with Dad, while Charlie Ashford hiked one foot on the running board of his pickup truck and talked with Hamp Moss about the work they were doing on the farm; but before the boys could finish playing together Dad was calling Byron to come on and leave.

Byron had celebrated his tenth birthday just last month. DeLane Moss was three years older than Byron, and Alvin Moss was two years younger than Byron.

The three boys sat on the front porch for a while. Byron felt an excitement in being at the Mosses' house without Mother or Dad or Hattie around. "Are we gonna play tag?"

"Hit's too blamed hot fer tag, Byron." DeLane always decided what they would do. "We'uz fixin' to go to the river whenever Miss Reen brung you."

"The river! Dad said I mustn't ever go near the river."

"Hush up. Maw'll hear."

"Are you going swimming?" Byron's eyes were round with fear.

"No, we was jus' goin' fer a walk to look at hit." DeLane cut his narrowed eyes over toward Alvin, who was dozing with half-closed lids in the heat and spoke in a shrill, mocking voice.

"Hit's too hot fer walkin' on the road." A fly crawled across Alvin's upper lip as he spoke, and Byron wished he would brush it away. Alvin stretched.

"We better tell Maw. You comin' er not, Byron?" DeLane swung up the leg that had dangled off the edge of the porch and pulled himself up by the post and went inside. "Dally? Ho, Dally? Where're you?" Byron followed him inside. "Alvin and Byron and me's gonna walk over to where Pa's a'plowin'."

Dally shifted the plug of tobacco back and forth from her bottom to her top lip nervously. "You oughter'n to call me by my given name. I'druther y'all stayed around the house."

"Byron he wants to see the mule he's a'plowin' with."

Dally eyed DeLane cautiously again. "Well, don't be gone more 'an an hour."

Byron followed DeLane and Alvin, who walked slowly and said nothing until they passed the barn. "We're goin' a'swimmin' in the river. You promise you ain't gonna tell on us."

"That's dangerous. Dad says grown men can get swept away in the current and be pulled down by a whirlpool and die."

"Hit ain't over yer head lessen they's a washout. You can hold onto roots on the bank and test out the bottom. You promise not to tell, or we'll go on back." The light from DeLane's green eyes held Byron like a vise.

"I promise, but I'm not gonna swim. Dad says grown men who are good swimmers can get drownded in that river."

"That's jist when the water's up."

"Well, I'm not gonna swim in it."

"Suit yerself."

The thought of taking off his clothes in front of DeLane and Alvin terrified Byron as much as his fear of the river current. He was not really hunchbacked. The lump was a deformity in his spine between his shoulder blades. ("Fortunately, it doesn't tilt his head forward. He can stand erect. It's hardly noticeable with his clothes on," he'd heard his mother say to people many times. Even when they went swimming at Smith's Lake, Mother brought along a t-shirt with his bathing suit so that no one would see his back.)

By the time the boys reached the river the sweat streamed down their faces and arms and legs, and their shirts stuck to their backs. They tasted the dust and the heat of the road in the salty sweat on their lips. The big stalks of river cane stood on the bank, almost as tall as the trees; and they rustled in the breeze with a hollow clacking like dried bones.

For years the people of Davis County had called it Canebrake Beach, because a great quantity of white sand had washed in front of the stand of canes. Over the years neighbors had come in their wagons and later in their pick-up trucks and asked the Ashfords' permission to haul sand from Canebrake Beach to lay the foundations of their homes. Most of the older homes in the northern end of Davis County were built with sand from Canebrake Beach. For most of the country folks, it had been the only beach they had ever seen (until their sons were drafted into the army and shipped abroad to foreign shores during the war or until much later, when even the cotton mill workers took annual vacations in Florida.)

Everywhere else along the river the bank plunged down six to twenty feet, and bushes and trees and tangled vines and blackberry briars prevented people from going close to the water. There were only a half dozen places on the Ashford farm where people could even get close enough to see the river. As the boys began to hear the gurgling slosh of the river through the pines, the brush and briars were still too thick to walk through. Only at Canebrake Beach was the riverbank low enough to allow people to slide out into the water for wading and swimming and fishing.

Today the river beckoned the boys into its cool, dark, mysterious water and murmured mysteriously. DeLane also beckoned to Byron from the water's edge. "You skeered o' swimmin'?"

"No, I know how to swim."

"You kin wade in behind me and keep a'holt o' me."

"I don't want to."

"Why not? What you skeered of then?"

"I don't want to take my clothes off."

"'Cause o' yer hump?" DeLane said it as matter of factly as though it were a cut that would heal in a few days, not something ugly and abnormal that would never go away. He said it in a tone that implied that everybody had a hump of some kind. Other people never mentioned it, except discretely to Mother when they thought that Byron wasn't listening. They tried not to look at it and quickly turned their eyes away when Byron became aware of their stares. "I don't kere what you look like naked. I jist hate you missin' out on swimmin'. Yer hump may be as ugly as Pa's ass, but hit ain't gonna hurt me none." DeLane had taken off his shirt, and Byron began slowly unbuttoning his shirt. Alvin glanced over at the lump on his back; but DeLane didn't even look up, as if he weren't even curious.

When they let their pants down, Byron noticed that he was different there, too. An acorn in a hull grew out of his groin, but theirs looked like the ends of snap beans, and hair was just starting to curl in black wisps on DeLane and seemed stranger and harder for him not to stare at than for Alvin not to look at his hump.

For several minutes they waded close to the sandy beach, never going deeper than knee high into the water. Then they moved beside the muddy bank downstream from Canebrake Beach. At first they held onto the top of the bank; then the bank became over a yard high above their reach; and they held onto the roots that jutted out of it.

"That there's a good root. You get a'holt of hit, Alvin; and I'll go test out the bottom." DeLane moved slowly away from the bank into the river. He squealed and shrieked. "Hey, hit's fun out here. Come on, Byron. Take a'holt of my hand and come on out, easy like. I'll catch you if'n hit gits over yer head. You can feel the water rubbin' around yer belly real good ou'chere."

Byron eased out into the river, holding onto first Alvin and then DeLane as he waded. He could feel the river pulling against him like hundreds of fingertips. No water had ever felt like the river's water. He shivered, and Alvin shivered as he slipped past him. As he waded deeper and deeper the water felt like cold hands reaching up his body. Above him the trees were dark and green, and below him the water was black. The sun shone far, far out in the middle of the river, beyond the edge of the trees' shade, farther than they could go, where the water was brown and golden and white.

Then Byron lost his balance, and the current pulled him under. His eyes and nose and mouth filled with the black cold water; and above him he could see shimmering green. He thought that he was about to die. DeLane's hand gripped his arm tighter and tighter, but the rest of him seemed to dissolve into the river. He felt that only the arm where DeLane clasped him was alive and still belonged to the earth. He was always aware of his hump, even when he was asleep; but now he felt that the river had washed it away into some black-brown, cold-shimmering watery grave.

DeLane and Byron were both in the current, but DeLane somehow got Byron onto his feet and held him around his stomach. Byron was gagging and fighting and clinging, but DeLane held him firmly and finally got them both to the bank. He dragged Byron up the steep incline and beat his back to clear the water out of him. He pressed his back just below the hump, and Byron stopped coughing. Then DeLane began rubbing the lump on his back, round and round, gently and firmly for a long time, the way the water had massaged his belly. It was the first time anyone had ever touched his hump like that. Byron smiled and no longer shivered. DeLane used his shirt to dry Byron and flick off the sand and wet dead river weeds from his stomach. When Byron began breathing normally again, DeLane burst into tears.

"If'n you'd of drownded, I'ud of drownded myself, too; and we'ud of been dead together."

Alvin stood naked beside them and looked on with terrified eyes and crossed arms and chattering teeth. Then they moved down the top of the riverbank and lay on the sand of Canebrake Beach until their clothes dried. Just before they stood up to dress, DeLane began rubbing the lump on Byron's back again and finished by squeezing it with his fingers. He smiled at the hump, as if it were something strange and amusing, perhaps like some odd animal dredged up from the bottom of the river. No one had ever been brave enough to touch Byron's hump that way before.

DeLane had saved Byron's life, and Byron repeated to himself over and over again, "DeLane saved my life; DeLane saved my life." Something joined DeLane to Byron at the river that afternoon, and Byron believed that they had become a part of each other's lives and would always belong to one another and would be best friends for as long as they lived.

## WINTER AND SPRING OF 1946

When the temperature dropped below freezing Mother would not let Byron go to the Mosses' house to visit because she was afraid that he would get a chill from playing with the boys. The winter was spent for the most part in Hattie's kitchen, for the kitchen in the big house belonged to Hattie like the library belonged to Dad and the dining room belonged to Mother. If Byron belonged in any room, it was in Hattie's kitchen. He was told a hundred times every week to "go see Hattie in the kitchen," when Mother and Dad grew bored with him and bothered by his questions.

Hattie sometimes came into the rest of the house, in spring to wash the windows and every Tuesday to dust the furniture and help Mother make up the beds with clean sheets; but she never seemed to belong in the other rooms, and Mother always seemed to borrow the kitchen from Hattie when she went in to cook something special there. It was Hattie's kitchen; and Mother was alone there only after supper, washing the dishes, always in the twilight without a light on, as if someone might see her in the room where she didn't belong. The kitchen seemed to be an extension of Hattie's house more than it was a part of the big house. There was not a real kitchen in

Hattie's house. She took most of the food for her family across the garden from the big house in the evenings when she left.

Hattie's daughter, Tancy, and stepson, Elmo, lived with her. Tancy was not much older than Byron, maybe about DeLane's age; but Elmo was a grown man, almost as old as J. W., DeLane's brother, who was away from the farm in the army during the war. Byron didn't like to go to Hattie's sweltering house in the summertime with its low tin roof and only the front door and two windows for ventilation, but he liked to go during the winter when a blaze crackled in the fireplace and especially when Elmo cooked over the hearth. Although Hattie cooked most of their food in the kitchen of the big house, sometimes Elmo fried fish and baked corn still in the shucks and sweet potatoes in their jackets and popped popcorn and made coffee in the fireplace.

In the late autumn Hattie's bedroom was filled with cotton, because her house was right beside the big cotton field; and Hattie and Tancy would have to sleep in the corner of the kitchen of the big house until the cotton was sold. It was cold in Hattie's house until Dad sold the cotton, because he would not let them build a fire until the cotton was out of the house for fear that it would be ignited. Byron liked to lie in the cotton to keep warm and bounce and roll inside it and listen to Elmo whistle. The day they took all the cotton away Dad would give Hattie some ham and sweet potatoes and bacon and popcorn, and Byron would spend all afternoon watching Elmo cook in the fireplace and have the best supper of the whole year with them that night.

Mother let DeLane and Alvin come up to the big house to play with Byron in the winter, but she made them stay inside. They often cut pictures out of magazines and newspapers on the big gray table in Hattie's kitchen. The Mosses used all the newspapers they had for putting on their walls—all the walls of their house were covered with layers and layers of newspapers for insulation. Dally never used paper for reading or writing, but she valued paper for putting on her walls to keep out the cold and for drying her garden seeds on and then for folding around them in packets and for wiping herself at the privy when there was enough left over from the walls and the seeds, (so that she didn't have to use corn cobs soaked soft in a bucket.) Mother gave Byron all the paper he wanted for cutting up and drawing. Byron and DeLane and Alvin even drew pictures with crayons; and DeLane liked doing such childish things, because he'd never had any crayons when he was a little boy, even though he was now almost fourteen years old.

The shirts the Moss boys wore were made out of flour sacks, and the sacks had patterns printed on them. DeLane had one shirt with a big purple flower on the back, but no one ever teased DeLane about his purple flowered flour shirt nor about anything else, because most people were afraid to rile DeLane. None of the shirts had collars, and the sleeves were uneven and floppy.

Alvin's teeth were crooked; and when he colored pictures or cut out photographs from magazines, his eyes crossed. Mother told one of her friends that DeLane was the only younger Moss boy with any real grace and promise and "absolutely marvelous" with younger children; but Hattie didn't approve of DeLane visiting in her kitchen. If Mother wasn't in the kitchen when DeLane arrived, Hattie would try to keep him from coming in the back door.

"He gonna teach Byron nastiness."

"What do you mean by nastiness, Hattie?"

"Jus' nastiness, Miss Reen. Jus' pure nastiness."

Byron winced when Hattie and DeLane began fussing and feuding. Their words caused him even greater pain than the angry words between Mother and Dad.

"Don't pay no 'tention to that ol' Nigger womarn."

"Who you sassin', you no good nasty boy. You get outa my kitchen with you' ugly talk."

"No Nigger womarn is gonna tell me what to do."

Hattie snatched a pile of movie stars' photographs that DeLane had cut from an old magazine and ripped them up and wadded them into a ball in her hands. DeLane began to cry. "You tore up my purties!"

Hattie's face changed from anger to helpless frustration. For a moment she looked as if she might hug DeLane as she would have held Byron when he cried. Then she looked as if she might slap him as she sometimes slapped Tancy when she was complaining and whining in a shrill voice. Her face went back and forth between frustrated pity and stern anger like the pendulum of the grandfather clock in the front hall. Finally she opened the back door and stormed out. "I'ze goin' to my house for a spell."

DeLane smiled when the door closed behind her and wiped his eyes with his sleeve. "I reckin we showed her who's boss."

J. W. came home just before the land was plowed under for the winter, and Dad said it was a good thing. If Hamp had tried to farm by himself for one more year, the crops would have been ruined for sure. The Mosses planted and harvested almost all of the row crops, the cotton and wheat and corn; and Elmo, Hattie's stepson, tended some of the vegetable gardens and took care of the cattle. Dad worked with both families from time to time, but mostly he supervised their labor. (Even after he grew up, Byron could never figure out how Dad divided up the income from the farm between the three families, but everyone had food and shelter and clothes, and his family's lot didn't seem to be grander or better than that of the white and black tenant families except for living in a larger house.)

J. W. had served in the army in Ohio during the war, not across the ocean fighting the Japs and the Nazis, even though Hamp and Dally told people that was what he was doing and probably believed it themselves. Ohio seemed almost as far away to them as Germany and Japan. J. W. was Dally's oldest child except for the baby she'd lost. Even when J. W. came in from the field and took off his straw hat and wiped his face with his bandanna, his hair was combed slick against his head with a part almost in the middle. His face was like a little boy's, and he smiled almost all the time.

The fields looked different that year. The earth was plowed deep, and it lay back wet and brown. The dry shallow spots and tufts of weeds and stubble that Hamp had left in the fields, (which looked like the stubble on his face,) couldn't be found after J. W.'s plowing. The rows were straight and close together and ran all the way to the bushes. Dad told Byron that J. W. had been their salvation. "I don't believe we could have gone on another year with Hamp doing the plowing and harvesting. You'll have to deal J. W. one of these days, and he may put you on your mettle."

When Byron asked Dad what he meant, Dad didn't answer him; and his face took on a strange dreamy look as if he'd seen a vision. Dad didn't stop the truck as often and step outside on the running board and take the flask from below the seat and drink with his back toward Byron after the war was over. The redness lightened in his face; but the curly ringlets of hair around his ears began to turn grey, even though his moustache stayed brown.

When the telephone rang after eight o'clock at night, it was probably bad news, and if anyone called after ten o'clock it was "bound to be" bad news. In the winter the phone ringing late at night was even more frightening than amidst the summer sounds of frogs and birds and crickets. The winter that Byron's uncle died, (the husband of Dad's sister,) the ringing echoed through the still, shut-up house and broke the silence like glass shattering. Dad shivered in the cold while Mother searched for a coat to put on over her bathrobe and then listened from a dark doorway to the fright in Dad's voice in the coldness.

Byron turned over in bed and tried to decide whether he was curious enough to get out on the cold floor rather than go back to sleep. Then he heard Mother say, "What'll we do with Byron?" He slowly climbed out of bed, so that whatever was happening wouldn't be decided without consulting him. "We can't leave him here, and we can't take him with us."

"I reckon we'd better take him down to Dally's. She'll keep him."

"Do I have to get dressed?"

"No. Just slip on your shoes and socks and I'll get together some clothes for you to put on tomorrow morning." His mother was stuffing some of his clothes into a cloth bag as she spoke to Byron.

The grass and the ground were frozen and crunched under their feet like shards of glass breaking. Whenever Dad drove the car at night before, there were always lights along the way, electric lights behind them in the big house and the flickering of a candle at Hattie's and the rich, dull glow of oil lamps at the Mosses'; but that night they left from darkness and went toward darkness, and not even a star shone out. The headlights of the car searched the emptiness, and Byron wondered if the road would end suddenly and toss them into a great black hole.

Byron had never seen the Mosses' house in the dark, and the gray, unpainted boards slumped in the night like the corpse of a house. The hounds ran out from underneath the porch barking and breaking the solid blackness into sharp splintered fragments, as the telephone had shattered the silence inside the big house. Hamp looked out a window with a flashlight; then Dally came onto the porch carrying an oil lamp and wearing a nightgown that came down around her ankles. Her light brown hair fell down around her cheeks almost to her waist; and she looked like a witch until they got out of the car and could see her fat red face in the lamplight. Not even one coal glowed in the fireplace—it must have been very late; and Dally moved Alvin over in his bed. He groaned and turned over but never woke up, and soon Byron was asleep beside him in the same kind of warm furrow he'd left in his own bed.

Byron was awakened when Dally began moving pots around in the kitchen, but he stayed in bed until he heard the popping of meat frying in a skillet and smelled coffee and the acrid homemade bacon. Alvin didn't wake up as Byron dressed, even though he put his pants and socks on underneath the covers to keep warm. Dally was setting the table with plates and enamel cups with black chips like scabs on the edges. DeLane was asleep on a cot behind the kitchen table with the covers pulled up over his ears. Dally looked at Byron standing in the kitchen doorway and said as little as usual except with her eyes. She never wasted precious words saying "Good morning" or "Good-bye" or asking useless questions about how you slept or how you were feeling when she could see from your face that you'd slept hard and didn't see any signs of peakedness about you.

"DeLane, git up and git dressed." DeLane let out a low friendly growl and turned over, and Dally turned toward him. "Git up, I say." He pulled back the covers and stood up, completely naked with his mother facing him. She turned her face away in sour disgust. "Fer shame. Shame on you with Byron here lookin' a'chu."

"You told me to git up, ol' womarn. What's he doin'here anyways. Hey-yo, Byron." Now he had the shape of a man in his arms and legs and chest, even though his waist was still thin like a boy or a woman; and a line of hair ran up to his navel, and a thicket of hair circled where he swelled out to his man's full length. He stretched and yawned and grinned and raised his middle finger toward Byron good humoredly. And Byron said his morning prayer for the first time, which he repeated day after day for months and even years afterward: "God, let look like DeLane when I grow up."

Byron wondered how DeLane could stand the cold; but DeLane liked being naked, even in the wintertime. "Git your clothes on er I'll tell J. W. Shame on you." But J. W. came in the back door from the outside on the word *shame*, red-faced from the cold. Byron knew that DeLane would be whipped, especially since he had been present to witness the argument between DeLane and his mother. When J. W. took the razor strop out of the cabinet, DeLane pleaded with him for mercy; and J. W. relented somewhat and took off his belt to use instead, probably also because Byron was present looking at them with appalled eyes and bloodless lips. J. W. made DeLane bend over and struck him until dark red stripes appeared on his buttocks. Byron winced as if it were his own flesh that was being struck; and with every crack of the belt against DeLane's skin Byron thought, *I hate J. W. Moss. I hate J. W. Moss for hurting DeLane. He's just showing off for me, and I hate him.*

In the early spring, when the buds, still more brown than green, had begun to pop out on the giant oaks in the cow pasture north of the big house, Dad gave Byron a horse that he named Prince Hal; and as soon as he learned to ride well enough, he was allowed to go to the Mosses' house by himself. When he had ridden to their house with Dad in the pick-up, Dad always called him in a few minutes, before the first person was even caught in tag, unless DeLane was *it*, because he caught everyone in a few seconds and never would have had to be *it*, if he hadn't come close with his daring taunts.

Now almost every afternoon after school Byron rode Prince Hal down to the Mosses' house and stayed for an hour or two. Dally worked all the time, and the boys had their chores to do. Sometimes Byron tried to help them, but he learned mostly to keep out of their way. DeLane slopped the hogs with everything that was left from all the cooking pots and pans. Alvin drew water out of the well with a wooden bucket on a long rope suspended from the wench, and twice a day DeLane carried it to the barn to water the hogs and also the mule and the cow when they were penned up. The chickens found their own water in the branch behind the house. Dally watered the tomato plants and the flower beds—the rest of the garden was dependent on God—and swept the dirt yard with a stick broom once each morning and once in the evening. The Mosses didn't have any grass in their yard, and all around their house was hard packed clay without a single weed or blade growing in it.

Dally was continually chasing the chickens out of her garden. They were different colors, and one of the boys' games involved crawling under the Mosses' house where the chickens scratched and fluttered in the dust; the boys banged against the floor of the house to run them out, cackling and flapping against one another. Sometimes the hens laid their eggs under the house in little smoothed out holes in the dust instead of on the floor of their roost; and when they broke an egg from the boy's game of running them out, Dally cried in frustration; but she didn't punish them when Byron was involved.

Dally cooked in the mornings and cleaned in the afternoons. She washed clothes in a tub in the yard once a week, and she made all her dresses and all the men's shirts. She dug in the garden and hoed weeds out of the corn and cotton fields with a bonnet on her head. The younger boys didn't have to work in the fields, except at planting time and at the harvest, when they picked the cotton and the corn; but sometimes they would go to the fields and hoe with the rest of the family. One afternoon when Byron got to their house, Dally had just taken a dip of snuff and couldn't tell him where the boys were. J. W. came in wiping the sweat off his face with his bandana.

"The young'uns they got work to do today, Byron. They ain't got time to play with you. This here farm is gonna be yourn someday. You better be findin' out about how hit runs. Did you ever think about that?"

"No. I'm not going to be a farmer." Byron had never conceived the thought before, but it became a sudden resolution that stuck in his mind.

"What's gonna become of hit then?"

"I don't know." Byron decided that he didn't like J. W., who smiled at him and kept wiping his face over and over, as if he knew what Byron was thinking and what Byron would say and do before he said it and did it.

After the Mosses began the spring planting DeLane didn't have time to play with Byron in the afternoons. Once again Byron began going to Hattie's house after school and sitting on the porch with Elmo until dusk.

The days were getting warm; and Byron began to feel the beads of sweat on his face and neck and sides.

Byron had learned to swagger, from watching DeLane, and to stick out his rear end and throw back his shoulders and walk bow-legged and put his fingers through his belt loops as he walked. Charlie thought it was funny, and Irene thought it was cute. "He's a good-looking boy, Charlie, in spite of his posture."

"It's not posture, Reen. It's a deformity. You might as well call it what it is."

"Yes, but it's hardly noticeable with his clothes on. He has a good face. It's strong and tender. I never saw a child's face combine as much strength and gentleness as Byron's, even if he is my own son."

"That's so, Reen. And I do love to see him strut."

"DeLane's been a good influence on him . . . given him pride in himself. I know DeLane drives Dally out of her mind with his independent streak. He's the only one of the Mosses that really has a mind of his own, and I believe that's good for how Byron thinks of himself. Do you think he'll ever marry, Charlie? Do you think his back will hold girls off?"

"I think he'll be all right, Reen. You worry too much over him." Then Charlie heard Byron eavesdropping from the hall. "Byron, that you? Come in here. Go down and tell Elmo I want him to clean out the chicken house tomorrow morning."

Whatever DeLane said was "law and gospel" to Byron, and one thing DeLane was sure about: no white boy should hang around black people. Sometimes Byron would repeat Mother's words, "Colored folks are people, too"; but DeLane and Alvin would argue with him and say that they were more like animals than people; and finally Byron would agree that they were almost worthless and that a hundred colored people were not worth as much as one white man; but he couldn't believe his own words, because he knew that Elmo and Hattie were good and that he loved them. What DeLane said about planning to beat them up every chance he got bothered Byron; and he never repeated those words, even with his fingers crossed. Of course he never used the word *Nigger* around Mother and Dad; and even when he used it to impress DeLane, he felt bad and guilty, as though something tasted bitter in his mouth.

Tancy was sitting on the front porch stringing beans, and Byron could see Hattie though the door. "Is Elmo home?"

"He washin' hisself at the back."

"I'll go find him." Byron started through the house to the back porch.

"Hey, you can't go back dere wid him naked." Tancy's voice was even higher pitched and shriller than usual.

"He's a man, ain't he?" Byron stuck out his rear end and fastened his fingers into his belt loops and swaggered past Tancy through Hattie's back door; but Elmo wasn't naked, not like DeLane had been on the morning that Uncle Percy had died. He wore a pair of patched baggy blue shorts that used to be Dad's and had soaped the upper part of his body and was rapidly rinsing it off by dashing water out of a battered tin wash pan that sat on the shelf where all the washing was done. The water was cold, but Elmo didn't shiver as Byron had shivered in the river. The wood of the shelf was rubbed and polished to a slick, silvery gray by the soapy water poured over it hundreds of times. Byron had never seen Elmo without the baggy clothes that hid his form and shape. Byron knew that Elmo was strong; Dad had said, "He's stout as a mule—stouter than J. W. even"; but Byron thought that he would have had a shapeless strength like J. W.'s.

"You're strong!"

"Ha'd wouk make a man strong." Elmo stooped down and poured the wash pan of water over his head, and the water glistened on his face, and Byron saw his features for the first time. His face and body showed a strength that would last and never become flabby—not like the plastic dolls of men that could be squeezed out of shape in middle age because nothing was inside them. Then he patted himself dry with a towel, in rapid, brisk movements, because it was chilly, even though it was a late spring morning. "'scuse me not habin' my clothes on."

"It doesn't matter. I've seen lots of men with nothing at all. I'm a boy, so what's the difference?"

Elmo looked at him sadly and said with his eyes, *because I'm a colored man and you're a white boy.* "Un-huh."

"I'll never be strong like you."

"Why's that?"

"Because of the lump on my back."

"What you is on the inside is mo' important that what you is on the outside. Is you gonna be able to love people? Dat's bein' strong on the inside."

"Do you think you're strong on the inside, Elmo?"

"Yes sir. I believe I is. I believe I be strong on the inside and be lovin' to mos' people."

For a moment Byron thought, *I'd like to be Elmo's friend like I'm DeLane's friend*; but the thought lasted only an instant, because he wanted DeLane to stay his friend more than anything else in the world; and DeLane might not want to be his friend, if he was Elmo's friend, too.

Elmo put on his baggy clothes and disappeared into them, like a man who hides and keeps his real identity a secret, for fear that the world may discover who he really is.

"Did you come t' tell me somephin'? You don't come 'round here jus' to set around wif me much in the daytime the las' little while."

"Yeah. I came to tell you that Dad wants you to clean out the chicken house tomorrow." And Byron added all on his own, "And be sure you get started on it bright and early," which is what he thought DeLane would want him to say and be proud of him for saying, even though he knew that Elmo began his work as the sun was rising and worked harder than any other man on the farm.

## SUMMER OF 1946

The first small green buds began to open into fragile leaves on the giant oaks in the pasture on the north side of the big house, when Hattie's nephews from Detroit came to visit because their mother was sick. Zed was about Alvin's age, and Early was a year older than Byron.

At first Byron approached them cautiously. They asked him if he wanted to walk with them down to the creek to see the fish. The next afternoon they caught some minnows and dug up some worms from the back of the hen lot and went fishing. Early and Zed could see fish in the water quicker than Byron could spot them and find all kinds of things under rocks. They knew about the haints in the woods and what haints' caves looked like. Sometimes the three of them would lie beside the creek on the big flat gray rock and look up at the sky through the trees, and Zed and Early would point to a bird or a squirrel without saying a word or making a sound, and they would all watch for an hour.

Early almost always walked on his tiptoes. He said it was "Injun walkin'" so that nobody could hear him, but he walked on his tiptoes even on the road when they began to get excited as they talked together. He could run faster than any boy Byron had ever seen. Byron thought Early might even be able to beat DeLane, who was almost a man, in a race; but DeLane wouldn't race a colored boy.

"Don't you want to play tag or hide-'n-seek or something? DeLane and Alvin and I play that all the time, and red rover, too."

"Naw. It tire me out and ain't no fun. I rather race or fish or look for things in the woods." Zed yawned.

Early's eyes opened wide. "Hattie say there's Injun gold buried in the woods along the creek. She tell us while we was visitin' to look under rocks and we might see a sign of it." They turned over a thousand rocks without ever finding a trace of the treasure left by the Chrokees.

One afternoon while they were lying on the big flat gray rock beside the creek watching a kingfisher dive and retrieve fish and fly back up onto a branch, Early raised up on his elbow and looked at Byron. "What's that ball on your back? Does it hurt you much?"

Byron also lifted himself onto his elbows and faced Early. "I was born like that. No, it doesn't hurt me at all. It's just there."

"Will it go away?"

"No. I'll always be like this."

Early pulled up Byron's shirttail. "Can I touch it?"

Byron said, "Okay," and thought, *Maybe Early will rub it and massage it like DeLane. Maybe Early will be a friend to me like DeLane.* But Early's fingers touched him as if they were afraid, lightly, as if they might need to run away. He thought that Early's fingers were curious and repulsed, like the glances of the strangers who stared at him.

"That's enough." Byron pushed Early's hand away and pulled down his shirttail.

Mother had told Byron you must never ask people about the way their names sound or the way they look and not stare at them or appear too interested in anything odd about them, as she would glance away from Byron's back—and he could feel her eyes forcing themselves away from him in the same way other people's eyes were often fixed on him—so he asked Hattie in the kitchen, when they were alone, where he could ask anything or say anything even about colored people's secrets and white people's euphemisms, "That's a funny name. Why do you call him Early?" Byron thought it would have been impolite to ask Early himself, just as impolite as it had been for Early to ask him about the lump on his back.

"He was born befo' the time. Little bitty thing. Nobody thought he'd live till frost. So we call him Early."

"It was a premature birth." Byron spoke confidently, like a learned tutor to poor, old ignorant Hattie. He had heard Mother talking about a baby born before the full nine month's term in its mother's stomach just a few days ago. "Early was a premie." It was Mother's word, too, and the rhyme made him giggle: "premie Early."

"Not no *premie* now. He be the champeen in the foot races up at his school. Bigger an' faster an' stronger 'an any boy his age, an' him not big enough to fill up my slipper when he was born."

"Early's a nice name. It's not so funny when you get used to it." Byron thought of how Mother had told him that DeLane was named for President Roosevelt, whose middle name was something like what the Mosses called their middle son.

"It fit. Like lots of things, it outgrowed the reasonin' for the way it begin, and now . . . it just fit him. He be Early. Like a bright and mornin' star. He be Early."

Mother said she wished that Zed and Early would stay on to be Byron's playmates because he got so worn out with the Moss boys that his side hurt and he couldn't sleep at night. She thought that the Moss boys played too rowdily, and someday he would get hurt in one of their rough-house games. Byron asked Alvin to go fishing with Early and Zed, but he said he was "not about to play with no Niggers." Byron preferred Early and Zed's company to Alvin's anyway. It wasn't any fun playing with Alvin unless DeLane was with them, and now DeLane had to work almost all the time.

On Sunday afternoon Mother and Dad were sitting in the swing on the front porch, as they did almost every Sunday afternoon. Mother had helped Hattie make the potato salad as soon as they had come home from church, and right after lunch she had told Hattie to go on back to her house. Mother even washed the Sunday dinner dishes because Hattie had company, members of her family who had come to take Early and Zed back to Detroit. They could hear Hattie's company laughing and talking across the garden all the way to the big house. Hattie and Tancy and Elmo never talked loudly when they were by themselves, but today their voices went on for hours and hours, and they all seemed to talk and laugh at once.

Dad dozed and nodded as they rocked in the porch swing, but Mother began talking in a loud voice to Byron, probably in order to wake Dad up. "How is DeLane, Byron? I haven't seen him lately."

"Fine."

"Is he still your most special friend?"

"Yes'um. But he works all the time now. He won't have time to play till the crops are laid by. I like playing with Early and Zed, the little Nigger boys visiting Hattie, better than just with Alvin. He's no fun just by himself."

"Please don't use that word, Byron. They're people on the inside just like anyone else."

"Yes'um. I like 'em, but DeLane and Alvin won't have anything to do with 'em."

"When you're older, we'll talk about this, Byron." Mother began pulling her lips in over her teeth, as she did when she was upset. "Just try to be friends with all of them. Try to be nice to everybody. It's very, very important. That's all I can tell you now." She stood and started into the house. "Goodness, they're having a big time down at Hattie's."

The loud voices continued to cascade across the garden. Then there was silence, and Byron heard Tancy scream. Dad said, "I'd better go over and see what's going on at Hattie's." Byron hid behind the bushes beside the front porch, because he knew that if asked to go with Dad he would say, "You stay here" and if Mother saw him following Dad, she would say, "You come back here."

All the people from Hattie's house were out in her yard. Zed and Early were crying. Blood streamed down Early's face from his temple where he'd been hit on the side of his head with a rock, and Tancy kept screaming in her shrill voice, "DeLane, he done it. It was that DeLane."

Dad asked them what he had done and what the fight was about, and Zed answered, "DeLane he say we better stay in Hattie's yard 'cause we don't have no business bein' nowheres else. He say if we come pas' the barn he whoop our ass. We jes' gone down to the creek to see our minnow baskets, and DeLane he lyin' in the bushes waitin' fo' us. He throw this here rock and hit Early in the head; and when I yell, he come and knock me down and say if I tell on him he gonna kill me."

"Nobody's goin' to kill you, boy. DeLane won't hurt you anymore."

Hattie's face was squeezed up like a baby's face about to cry. "I didn't see no harm in them fishin'. I hope you don't objec' to them catchin' a few minnows out'a the creek, Mista Charlie."

"God put the fish here for all of us, Hattie. They don't belong to me any more than to DeLane. Anybody stays on this farm has as much right as anybody else to fish in the creek and the river. I just don't want anybody's a stranger trespassing over my land, but folks staying here have a right to go fishin'."

Dad brought Early up to the big house, and Mother took him to the hospital to be doctored. Dad sent Byron to the Mosses' house on Prince Hal to tell J. W. to get himself up to the big house right now. When J. W. came in Dad was angrier than Byron had ever seen him. "I want you to tell everybody in your family that I'll not have people throwin' rocks at other people on this farm, not at those who live here, not at those who visit here. I won't stand for it. You listen to me and you hear me well. I won't stand for it." J. W. was very humble and apologetic. He looked down and shook his head and toed the floor with his right foot.

Dad was sick from Monday until Saturday. He vomited and couldn't walk without leaning on something. Byron had never heard Dad give anyone an order before, not Mother, not him, not Hattie's family, and not any of the Mosses, until he made his demands clear to J. W. Moss. Byron remembered Dad's lips saying, "I won't stand for it." He wished that he could see Dad say, "I won't stand for it," just one more time, even if Dad said it to him, although he still believed it was an accident and DeLane hadn't really meant to hurt Early.

As the summer days grew hotter and heavier with humidity Byron had a hard time thinking up ways to get the Moss boys to go swimming with him in the creek, especially ways to persuade DeLane, because he could go swimming anytime he wanted to, even in the river; and nothing was any fun without DeLane along anyway. Byron let DeLane and Alvin ride with him on Prince Hal to the river, because DeLane wanted to, even though he knew that the three of them were too heavy for the little pony. Prince Hal sweated and panted on the road.

They got off to give Hal a rest and walked along on the white sand of Canebrake Beach. Byron was afraid and excited by the sounds of the river. He had tasted death there, and it lured him back; but even greater than the daring adventure of swimming in the river current was his hope that DeLane would touch the lump on his back again and grin at him and tell him they were still friends.

They took off their clothes and waded into the water near the white sand of Canebrake Beach, never venturing far from the bank into the deep water of the river. Alvin stared and glanced away from Byron as other people did, as he had done last summer; but DeLane treated him the same way he had last summer, like he was a normal boy.

"Let's us swim acrost the river." DeLane's eyes sparkled, but both Alvin and Byron knew that he was joking.

"I ain't lettin' nobody take no chances this here time." Alvin's sharp, pointed chin lifted with firm defiance.

"Did ol' Byron skere you las' summer, Alvin?"

"You near froze my tail off takin' all my clothes fer ta'els. You and him got dried off an' lef' me standin' up and shiverin' to death." Alvin grinned his good-natured grin. It was hard to believe that Alvin could ever be really angry with anyone.

They waded deeper into the water still hardly above their knees. If they hadn't splashed and pushed each other and squatted down, the rest of their bodies wouldn't have gotten wet. The river was cold, but their laughter was louder than the river's mysterious threatening murmurs. Occasionally Byron looked at the black and brown depths beyond the white sand and shivered with fear, but even the river seemed safe and benign as long as DeLane was there.

"We ourght'a do somethin' diff'rent to show we've swam in the river ag'in."

"We could write our names in blood."

"Naw, we done did that that a hundred times, and it aint' fittin' fer the river. Tell you what, we'll babtize one another, I seen 'em do it up at the crick by Philippi, and I'll show you how to."

DeLane showed Byron how to baptize him first; and when DeLane didn't come right up, Byron felt afraid, because he didn't want DeLane ever to be hurt or injured. Then DeLane baptized Byron, and he saw the whirling green and felt the cold water all around him except where DeLane's hands held him, and he remembered nearly drowning in the river last summer and how DeLane had saved his life. As they came up out of the water, DeLane splashed him and pushed him down, as he would do with any other boy; then he reached over and rubbed Byron's hump and grinned; and Byron thought that DeLane was the only person in the whole world who was not afraid and not ashamed to touch his hump, as if it were just like his shoulder or his arm.

J. W. guessed by their wet hair that they'd gone to Canebrake Beach and swum in the river, as they'd been strictly forbidden to do. J. W. made DeLane drop his pants and bend over a chair; and he hit him again and again, sucking in his great huge stomach and snapping the razor strop behind him and down against DeLane's flesh with a searing crack until the pink whelks swelled and turned red, like they had the morning Byron had spent the night at the Mosses' house after Uncle Percy died.

After it was over DeLane ran out to the Mosses' barn, crying from pain. Byron followed him and knelt beside him and told him that he was sorry. DeLane put his head on Byron's leg and cried for a long time.

"J. W. shouldn't treat you bad like that. He's mean."

DeLane stopped sobbing. "He ain't bad to me all the time. It's jest his way."

"I still hate him for being mean to you."

"Byron, yo're my goodest friend in the whole world."

## INTERVENING YEARS, 1947–69

In the winter of 1949, when Byron was fourteen years old, Dad died, only a few months after Hamp Moss died. DeLane dropped out of school and went to work in Atlanta, where he lived with a relative. J. W. Moss married Sylvia Jones, who had been a secretary in an insurance office since she finished high school as the valedictorian and most outstanding student in typing and shorthand that had ever graduated from Morganville High School. Dally took Alvin to live with her in Gilmer County, where she and Hamp had grown up and where she still had many relatives.

Before he died Dad had transformed most of the farm into a timber plantation and planted pine trees for the pulp industry to use in the paper mill that had replaced the cotton mill as the principal employer in Morganville. Elmo and Tancy moved to Detroit, where Elmo found a good job in an automobile plant through connections made by Zed and Early's parents.

As long as Mother lived in the big house on the farm Hattie continued to live in her little house behind the garden and help Mother with the cleaning and cooking, so far as she was able in her condition of advanced age and arthritis. J. W. and Sylvia Moss continued to live in the Mosses' tenant house, and J. W. managed the farm and supervised cutting the timber for Mother as he'd done for Dad.

During the summer of 1950 Mother decided that Byron would be enrolled in a boarding school in Tennessee, where her brothers had graduated and that she would move to an apartment in Morganville. Hattie moved to Detroit to live with Elmo and Tancy, but she hated that "cold, foreign land" and died within a year. A few months after Irene Ashford moved to an apartment in town, the big house where the Ashford family had lived for three generations was struck by lightning and burned to the ground.

BYRON BURST INTO THE small sitting room of Mother's apartment during his first visit home from the boarding school in Tennessee, when he heard Mother talking with J. W. Moss. He'd decided that he wanted to show J. W. how he much he disliked him. J. W. was sitting on the old settee that had belonged to Byron's great grandmother drinking a cup of coffee.

"Hello, J. W. What are you doing here?" Now J. W. wore khaki pants and a white shirt and a necktie with a windbreaker jacket when Byron came into town. He no longer wore the overalls that DeLane had despised.

"Hey-yo, Byron, I'm talkin' over some business with your Mama."

"J. W. is showing me where they plan to cut some more timber, son; and he thinks we ought to sell some of the land on the south end of the farm along the highway. He has the details here that we were talking about. Do you want to look over the figures with us?"

"No, thanks."

Charlie Ashford had sold some timber before he died, but the lumbermen hadn't begun cutting it. J. W. took care of overseeing the sawmilling for Irene Ashford, to be sure that the saw-millers didn't cut more than they'd bought and that they left the young trees and the sawmill roads in good condition.

"They's a real good market fer timber right now. I'd love to talk to you and your Mama about some more sales. Now that the war's over, they's a heap of people'll be wantin' to build houses."

"J. W. wants to buy their house and a few acres around it. They need more room now that they're starting a family. Did you know that Sylvia is expecting a baby?"

"No, I didn't know that." *And I couldn't care less*, Byron thought.

"Is it all right with you to sell some more of the land on the south end of the farm, Byron?"

"Sure, I don't care. 'scuse me."

"Wouldn't you like to take a look at the map, dear, to see what we're selling?" Byron glanced hurriedly at the map.

"Hit begins over here and goes to right about here."

"It doesn't take in the north pasture, does it?"

"Yes, dear. After we sold Prince Hall there didn't seem any good reason to keep it intact."

"Are you going to cut down the big oaks?"

"They'll make real purty floorin' for somebody."

"No! You can't cut down the oaks. Don't sell that part, Mother. Don't sell the big oaks or any of the land around Canebrake Beach, not yet, not for a while anyway."

"I've never known you to take any interest in the farm before, Byron. Maybe we'd better not sell anything else until we've talked it over."

"No. I don't care about any of the rest of it."

"That'll be fine, Miss Reen. Them old oaks is too big and cumbersome to be hardly worth foolin' with anyways. We wouldn't hardly make nothin' out of 'em."

"Just don't cut the old oak trees or sell the pasture behind the barn or the land around Canebrake Beach until you ask me first."

"Of course, dear. I'm glad you're taking such an interest."

After J. W. left, Byron blurted out, "I wish you'd find somebody else to help you besides J. W. Moss. I think he's mean, and I don't like him."

"You're quite wrong about him, son. J. W. takes very good care of us. If it wasn't for J. W. Moss, I wouldn't have any money to live on or to send you to school. In many ways J. W. has saved our lives."

"You don't know J. W., Mother. You don't know how mean he is. He whipped DeLane right in front of me, and I don't think he likes me much either." Then Byron went storming out of the room.

The summer that Byron turned sixteen J. W. arrived late one afternoon clutching soiled rolls of survey maps under his arm and holding dirty sheaves of other papers in tattered folders in his hand. He sat on the edge of the antique settee, as he always did, as if he was afraid that might break it if he leaned back. By now he was becoming wealthy trading timber and starting his own lumberyard with clients all over Davis County, not just from the trees cut on the Ashford farm. He was a busy man; but he always accepted a cup of coffee from Irene Ashford, because he didn't want to be rude.

Irene echoed Byron's frequent protest, "I do hope you won't put up any more of those cheap, trashy stores and beer joints on the south end of the farm."

J. W. nodded his head sadly in his customary way. "I hope not, Miss

Reen; but I jus' divide hit up in lots and sell hit. They ain't a way to make a livin' farmin' no more, as you well know yerself. Hit shore hurts me to see hit built up with sich like places though."

Byron's stomach soured at J. W.'s hypocrisy. He believed that J. W. would do anything he needed to do to turn a profit on their land.

As Irene initialed the papers and promised J. W. that she would stop by the lawyer's office in a day or two to sign the completed documents, Byron noticed a glint in her eye, something like revenge upon the land, which had been almost a mistress taking away her husband's affection and sapping his energy and tying her to a life imprisoned with debt, so that the dreams she'd dreamed as she'd stretched her long thin arms into the dishwater and looked out of the kitchen window into the dusk would never come true.

Byron thought that the land now belonged to people like the Mosses, who loved it only for the money it could bring them and cared for it in their own greedy way. They built four room concrete shotgun houses for poor black people to rent, and they established stores where poor white people could buy beer on credit and cafes where poor black people could buy cheap wine on credit, and interspersed between the houses and cafes and garages and filling stations were their aluminum-sided buildings where they produced burlap bags and concrete blocks and recapped tires.

Before he left, J. W. turned to Byron who was standing half in the hall, half in the doorway. "DeLane he's a' comin' down here next week, passin' through fer a visit to Dally. Reckin he'll be wantin' to see you."

Byron was so excited about the possibility of seeing DeLane again that he could no longer force his voice to stay low like Dad's. "What day's he coming?"

"They ain't no tellin' with DeLane."

"I don't suppose he'd really want to see me all that much anyway."

"That ain't so, Byron. He asts after you all the time. Ever' time he comes home, he asts if we've seen you or heerd anything from you."

"He does?" Byron's voice went completely out of control.

Byron waited expectantly for two weeks, but DeLane never came, and Byron gave up hope of ever seeing him again.

The next morning Byron borrowed Mother's car—he had just gotten his driver's license—and drove up to the north pasture where he'd ridden Prince Hal. Only a dozen great live oaks were left there now from the thick forest that Dad said had once covered the pasture when Byron's great-great-grandfather had settled here.

When Byron first arrived, the low ground fog hovered around the roots of the giant trees and covered the base of their trunks, so that their bare branches were levitated in the gray morning air, like black squiggly hieroglyphics suspended in the border of the sky. He waited for almost an hour inside the car to let the fog lift and the unreality of the scene pass. He'd come to see the old friends that he knew, not some phantoms created by tricks of the early light and vapors. As the sun rose, each tree stood out alone against the sky. Four or five were giants, greater and fuller than any forest tree had ever grown. Their huge gray branches were as large as the trunks of most trees. Two or three were as nearly perfect as a tree can be in shape and beauty; they had space to grow exactly as they pleased, and they'd survived the storms. Others were gnarled and twisted and bent over. One just above the creek was half destroyed by lightning. Gray branches pointed dead fingers downward to the white scar where the fire had torn half its trunk away, and yet its branches were still alive with green leaves on new shoots. It was bent over, twisted and cringing but still living. All its ugliness was exposed as it stood there alone and apart and unprotected. Byron thought that trees shouldn't have to grow apart and alone, without the protection of one another in a forest, even if a few of them could grow into perfect giants in the open space without the others nearby to crowd them.

Byron often pretended to talk to DeLane, because he thought that DeLane would understand how he felt about the farm and about how he still hated J. W. for being mean to them. If DeLane had come to visit them, he would have been able to talk to him as another teenager, no longer just a little boy; but he could still almost feel the spot on his arm where DeLane had held him in the river, and he wished that DeLane would touch his back again and grin at him as if it didn't really matter that it was humped.

Byron thought that if DeLane still lived here, he wouldn't feel as separated from the farm. He still sometimes prayed to be more like DeLane, not afraid of anything in the world, except maybe J. W.; and he hoped that when they did see each other again that DeLane would still be his friend, now that they were older. Occasionally Byron would remember DeLane's pale nakedness on the morning after Uncle Percy died, flashing for an instant across his memory with his raised middle finger and sparkling eyes, like light falling far out on the river at Canebrake Beach and then disappearing in the rippling current.

Mother had never knocked at Byron's bedroom door before that morning when he was masturbating, and his fear ran to panic. "Byron, why do you have your door locked? There's someone here to see you." He had gone too far to stop and furiously pulled and squeezed himself and then pulled his underpants over his wet penis and belly without drying them, in case the lock should fail and the door should fly open; but still he had no voice to answer her. "Are you all right? Are you asleep? What's the matter?"

"Who is it?"

"It's DeLane Moss."

"I'll be right there." He nervously folded the tattered cardboard he'd cut to fit around the photograph of the naked woman with her enormous breasts and soft amber pubic hair—he'd paid a fortune to buy it from an older boy at his school. He pushed it between the mattress and the box-springs, where he hid it from his mother. He dressed frantically, awkwardly, certain that DeLane would see a damp spot on his jeans or smell him and know what he'd been doing and tease him but afraid that if he took time to clean himself, DeLane would grow impatient and leave and be gone and lost forever and never be seen again.

DeLane was standing in the middle of Mother's living room. "Come on out and take a look. I got me a car."

DeLane's car was a green Studebaker the color of his eyes, (the model that broke the trend of beetle shaped sedans, that Jack Benny made jokes about on his radio show as not being able to tell whether it was coming or going, because the trunk was like the hood.)

On that one day Byron saw DeLane at the supreme height of his male beauty—no longer a boy, now fully a man, with a pale green tee shirt stretched tight around his biceps and over his chest and with a belt pulled tight around his thin waist, the only part of him still more like a boy than a man, so that his pants puckered into pleats. He was fully mature, not yet touched by any mark of age or flabbiness or softness. He wore white duck pants and white buck shoes and light green socks, the color of his tee shirt and his car, the color of his eyes.

DeLane seemed to be more molded from clay than chiseled from stone, as Byron remembered the shape of Elmo's very different manly body of rock. Grease made DeLane's hair iridescent; and Byron was aware of his own wiry hay-colored hair, the same color as Dad's, standing up in dry fuzzy waves and curls. He'd forgotten or not taken time even to comb it as he'd frantically dressed. Despite all his daily prayers, he'd failed to grow up like DeLane in any way whatsoever.

"I reckin yo're in high school now."

"Yeah. Are you goin' to school in Atlanta?"

"Naw. That jazz ain't fer me. I don't see as it'll do me no good. You got the smarts to make it work fer you though."

"You got a job?"

"Sure. I work at first one thing then t'other."

The silences in the desperate dialogues were painful for Byron. DeLane's world now seemed so different from his that there was a great distance between them. DeLane looked over at Byron with blank, open-lipped gaping, and seemed to recognize the hurt reflected in Byron's face. DeLane frowned and studied him for a few moments. "You ready fer a ride?"

"Okay. I'll go tell Mother we're leaving."

"I'll go with you and say goodbye to Miss Reen." As they walked through the apartment DeLane's eyes flitted from thing to another and seemed to take in every object. "Hit's shore been good to see you, Miss Reen."

"My goodness, DeLane, you've certainly grown up since we saw you."

"Yes'um. I'm near twenty year old now. Won't be no teenager much longer."

"DeLane and I are gonna ride around some."

Byron could tell that Mother was contemplating asking where they were going and how long they would be, but she glanced at Byron's still desperate face and thought better of it. "All right, dear."

DeLane revved the motor and tilted his ear down to listen. Then they moved off. He slowed down and crept along looking at people on the streets and then sped up so suddenly that Byron grasped the armrest; and then he slowed down again to look at a girl on the sidewalk. He turned on the radio so that they didn't need to talk. Byron was chilly from the sweat left on his skin after he'd masturbated in his bedroom before Mother called him, but DeLane kept the windows down and the radio turned up so loudly that they could be heard for several blocks. After riding around town for almost a half hour DeLane headed toward the country.

"Where are we goin'?"

"Nowheres particular. Jus' ridin'. You wanta go some'ers?"

"Not really. Are you headed up to the farm?"

"Not lessen you want to. I don't kere never to go back there. I got away, and I'm a'stayin' away."

They drove for a while longer without speaking. Then DeLane reached over and turned the radio down. "You gettin' any pussy?"

"No. I don't go out with girls much."

"You better git it while you can. They'll put out fer you down here in the country while yer a teenager. When you get older and live down in the city, you have to pay fer ever'thing you git."

Byron believed that DeLane could see him just as he'd been on his bedroom floor when Mother called him; and he suddenly determined that he had to be honest, even if DeLane hated him for it and would never have anything to do with him again. "I've never been with a girl like that. I wouldn't know what to do. Besides, no woman would ever fuck me." He couldn't remember ever using the word *fuck* before in a serious way, not just as a curse or a joke in the dorms at school.

"Hey, they ain't nothin' wrong with you. Yer prick's as good as anybody's. Maybe better from what I recollect. Yer hung right good, if'n I remember right."

"I donno . . . my back . . ."

"Hush that. I ain't gonna listen to no sich talk as that." DeLane pulled the car over on the gravel shoulder almost at full speed and braked to a stop that sounded like an explosion of rocks on the underside. He took a

piece of paper out of the glove compartment and drew a map to a house in
Rome where Byron could go and pay ten dollars. He wrote in a small, fine,
clear print, like an architect, with tiny square, perfect letters for the street
names. "They'll show you what all to do. Hit's pro'bly better to pay fer hit
yer first time, 'cause yo're real nervous. After that, hit comes natural. Hit
ain't no big deal. You've growed up to be right good lookin'. You'll git yer
share of pussy before yer done."

"Should I tell 'em you sent me?"

"If'n you want to. They know me right good. I been down there quite
a few times, but I wouldn't, though. Yo're good enough all by yerself. You
don't need to lean on me none. You might ast fer Marie though. She's a real
good piece of ass, and she'll have a plumb fit over you."

"Okay. I'll do it, if you think I'll be all right."

"Shore you will. When you goin'?"

"Sometime. I don't know."

"You go ahead and go this here weekend. You hear me. Friday night.
Promise me."

"Will you go with me?"

"Naw. You don't want me taggin' along. Not this time. It's some'um you
need to do all on yer own."

"Okay."

"Promise?"

"I promise."

"I'll call you up come Saturday. And if'n you didn't go git laid, I'll come
up here and whoop yer ass."

They drove for a long time and talked only occasionally. They stopped
for a hamburger and drove some more; and when they returned to Mother's
apartment, the streetlights had come on, so it must have been almost nine
o'clock. DeLane reached over and patted Byron on the back and rubbed
the lump and squeezed it in the old familiar way. "Ever'thing's gonna be
awright, Byron. Jist don't be skeered to try things out. You can have a heap
of fun in this here ol' world."

Byron was nervous when he asked his mother to use the car for a date
on Friday night. He told her that she wouldn't know the girl he was dating,

because she went to another boarding school in Tennessee and lived twenty miles away in Marietta. He made up a name and hoped he would never be found out. Irene was so pleased that he was having a date that she didn't ask many questions.

Byron located the house in Rome from DeLane's map, folded on the small piece of paper and taken out and read scores of times. The house was located in the edge of a black residential section of the town.

The woman who answered the door looked him over. He told her that he wanted a date, which was what DeLane had told him to say. She led him into a living room with a jukebox. The girls, about eight or nine who wandered in and out, wore tight shorts and black see-through blouses. Four or five were young. Several were very pretty. Two men, older than students, who seemed like day laborers or truck drivers, stared at the young girls; but the young girls frightened Byron. In spite of their exposed breasts, they look fresh and sweet and nice, like the girls from another boarding school who came to his school for dances. He thought they would reject him like the girls who didn't want to dance with him at school.

He noticed an older woman. She was thicker and slower than the young girls who flitted in and out of the room. She saw him staring at her—he was thinking of the mornings when he woke up and rubbed himself and nestled down against the pillow. The woman walked over to him. "You wanta buy me a coke?"

"Sure." She showed him the coke machine in the hall. They sipped their cokes out of a bottle, through straws provided in canisters on the tables, like the ones in the drugstore in Morganville.

"Do you know a lady named Marie?"

"A lady!" She laughed. "Well, my name's Marie. Why you asking, sugar?" He was about to ask if she knew DeLane; but she asked him first, "You go to college?"

"Yes ma'am," Byron lied, "I'm just a freshman up at the university in Tennessee."

"Unhuh," Marie answered knowingly. "You wanta dance?"

"Sure." She nestled against him closer than any woman ever had before. She seemed to press her body into his. "Hey, sugar, you're ready."

"I guess so."

"This your first time?"

Byron couldn't lie any longer. "Yes, ma'am."

"Well, don't you worry about nothin'. Marie'll take good care of you. Come on." They walked down the hall. "You got to pay me now. It's ten dollars for a quickie or twenty for the regular time. You better pay twenty if you got it, or the owner she's liable to come knocking at the door before we're finished, seeing as it's your first time and may take a while."

DeLane had told him it would only be ten dollars for the full treatment, but Byron thought that he shouldn't argue about the price. "Okay." He handed Marie the money. He trusted her. DeLane had told him to ask for her. She led him to a bedroom upstairs.

"Take off your clothes. I'll be back in a minute."

"Okay." Byron took off all his clothes except for his briefs and his tee shirt and sat in a chair waiting, as he'd waiting in the doctor's office for his physical exam at school. He waited a long time, about fifteen minutes, although it seemed hours to him. He was afraid that she wouldn't come back and would keep his money. In the frustrated waiting he lost the readiness that she'd felt when they were dancing. He thought she'd tricked him. Then she returned.

"Sorry to take so long. The owner she had to talk to me. She always picks the worst times."

"That's okay."

Marie undressed him and showed him how to do everything. She was patient and understanding. After they were linked together and began moving against one another, Byron felt the same pleasant sensation as when he masturbated and held a pillow against himself, but amplified by ten, maybe twenty times. Now he knew what the mysterious feeling of promise in his bedroom had meant.

After they finished Marie dried him. "We can lay here a little while if you want to. The old lady won't be comin' since you paid for a double. If you feel like it, we can even do it again."

"That would be great!"

"Does that hurt you?" Marie pointed to his back.

"No. It's just there. It doesn't hurt or keep me from doing anything I want to."

"It sure don't keep you from being a good lover. You're real good and gonna get even better with a little more practice. You have to come back regular and always ask for Marie. You like me, don't you?"

Byron raised himself on his elbow and kissed her cheek. "You're beautiful."

"Ain't you sweet. You wanta go again?"

"Oh yeah!" And the second time was even better than the first.

On his way home Byron kept thinking about how he was going to thank DeLane over and over when he called tomorrow. He laughed out loud. He sang. No matter what happened to him later, this had been the best night of his life. Marie had said that he was a good lover. She'd said he was a Cocacola king size, when he got his erection. He'd tell DeLane what she'd said on Saturday, tomorrow. He was as much a man as anyone, at least with a woman; and he owed it all to DeLane. There was no way that Byron could ever thank DeLane for what he'd done for him. DeLane was the best friend anyone could have in the whole world.

Byron waited all day Saturday and stayed awake until midnight, but DeLane never called him. Byron didn't see DeLane and didn't even talk with him again for almost fifteen years, but he kept the little piece of paper with the directions to the whorehouse in Rome folded up into a tiny packet inside his wallet for all those years, even though he never returned to Rome for a date with Marie.

AFTER GRADUATING FROM THE boarding school in Tennessee Byron went to Vanderbilt University, where he received a degree in English, and was accepted into the doctoral program. He was granted a Master's degree while he continued to work on his doctoral thesis and began teaching back at his old boarding school. He became the head of the English department there, and the work on his doctoral thesis seemed to have no end and less and less purpose. He'd begun dating a teacher at the school where they both taught, and he'd considered asking her to marry him.

Then in the spring of 1970 Irene Ashford was diagnosed with breast cancer. She was experiencing many other health issues, related to her age and infirmity—she'd been almost forty when Byron was born. Byron decided that he would spend the summer with her in Morganville and assess her situation as well as his own.


## THE SUMMER OF 1970 UNTIL THE SPRING OF 1971

On the second week of June, Byron sent his letter of resignation to his school in Tennessee. Irene Ashford would need regular radiation and chemo treatments for several months after her mastectomy, and Byron still needed time to decide what he wanted to do with the rest of his life. He regretted more than anything else resigning as an officer of the Urban League and putting aside his efforts to implement school integration in Tennessee. Since leaving Morganville the Civil Rights Movement had come to define his identity more than any other aspect of his work. Perhaps it countered his guilt or at least served as an antidote to his life as a boy growing up in a segregated society.

On the third week of June Byron received a telephone call from Kermit Stoner, the Superintendent of the Morganville City School System, (which was still separate from the Davis County School System). Kermit had been a friend of his father's for many years. He asked if Byron would meet him at his office at City Hall, and they made an appointment for Thursday afternoon.

"I hear tell you resigned from that boarding school up in Tennessee."

"Word travels fast. When did you talk to Mother?"

Kermit Stoner almost squeaked when he laughed. "About a half-hour before I called you up. I told Reen it wouldn't be any secret how you found out."

"And just what are you and Mother plotting."

"Byron, I'll come straight to the point. My high school principal's gone and quit on me. He took a job at some big school in the suburbs close to Atlanta. Here it is just two months till school starts, and I'm between a rock and a hard place. You think you might be interested in helping me out?" Kermit Stoner had been bald as long as Byron could remember. He looked his age, in his late sixties, although not any older. His skin hadn't wrinkled, and he had hardly enough eyebrows to turn gray, but his skull showed through the red skin of his face and scalp as it hadn't done a few years before.

"Help you out how?"

"Taking over as principal for the year. Reen said you'd decided to stay around so you could take her to her doctors."

"I've never worked in public school education, you know. All my experience has been in a private school."

"That won't be a problem. You'd be great for the job. Let me be honest with you; I'm sixty-seven years old. This will probably be my last year; I don't think I'm going to run for re-election. I'm looking for someone to get me through the year. "Course I imagine anybody'ud be glad to have you stay right on if you decide to, but I'm just concentrating on getting through this year, and I thought it just might help out both of us. I know you'll need time to take care of Reen, but we can be flexible about your schedule when you need to be with her."

"It's certainly an intriguing possibility, but do you really think I'm qualified?"

"'Course you are. I've done a little snooping." Kermit picked up a manila file folder and then laid it down on top of his desk without opening it. "Besides, I already know all I need to about you. I knew your Daddy right well."

"That may be the problem. I wonder if I'd fit in now."

"Why's that?"

"Well, people in Morganville would probably think I'm pretty liberal now, especially about racial issues. I've been very active in the Civil Rights Movement in recent years. That's not how people remember Dad."

"So you're a raving liberal now, are you? Well sir, I 'spect you got more of your Daddy about you than you think. Come on and take over the high school for me this year. I don't know any medicine better than the real world to dry up liberalism."

"I'll think about it."

"You do that, Byron. Only I don't want you to swing back too far, too fast. Liberals usually wind up Nigger-baiters, and I sho'ly don't none of that in my school."

"I don't think you need to worry about that, sir."

"I'm not worried about that nor anything else, Byron. You just take the job and agree to be my principal, and I'll not be worried about a single thing."

J. W. Moss continued to bring papers for Irene Ashford to sign almost every week. Now J. W. was a truly wealthy man. He'd torn down the old tenant house where he grew up and built a brick ranch style house on the branch only a few hundred yards from where it had stood. He'd replaced his khaki slacks and windbreaker jackets with polyester suits and carried colored silk handkerchiefs in their breast coat pockets, and Byron found him as contemptible as ever.

"Don't know if you heerd that DeLane he's moved back. You seen him yet?"

"No, I didn't know that. What's he doing?"

"He's got him a used car lot up on the south end of the farm, on a lot we bought from Miss Reen. What you and Miss Reen'ud call one of them trashy, junky-lookin' places, I reckin." J. W. chuckled; and Byron couldn't help joining his laughter, as if it no longer mattered what happened to the farm or what J. W. said and did. "You oughter go up and see him. He'd love to see you."

"I'll have to do that." Byron felt an unexpected surge of youthful expectancy. He wanted to see DeLane, but he was afraid that DeLane would not have changed in the same ways that he had. He cherished their childhood friendship, but he wondered if they could be real friends now after fifteen years apart, and he dreaded losing the memories of their attachment as boys when the reality of their present lives clashed.

Irene had been listening to Byron's conversation with J. W.; and when J. W. left, she asked if Byron didn't want to see DeLane, who had been his closest childhood friend.

"It's all in the past, Mother. DeLane's probably not the same person he was fifteen years ago. He and J. W. wouldn't accept black people then. I expect they're not much different now." He was aware of his own inner conflict, fearing that DeLane hadn't changed and that he'd changed in ways that separated them by an even wider gulf.

"People change. J. W.'s changed. You don't have all the answers with your bi-racial committees and your Urban League."

Byron remembered telling his mother about serving on the bi-racial faculty committee from Vanderbilt and Fisk and how a group of black and white graduate students and teaching assistants had gone together to a couple of the river restaurants and been arrested. They'd paid their fifty dollar fines and not been put in jail. He'd told her lest the next time he might be taken to jail and have his picture in the newspapers or on television, and she'd taken it calmly and without protest. "It's still a whole 'nother world down here."

"People change at their own pace. J. W.'s hired Negro men at his lumber yard and pays them the same wages as he gives white men. A lot of people give J. W. a hard time for treating colored people and white people the same. He's even put some Negroes over whites on some of his crews, and not everyone likes that. Not a bit. He's come in for quite a lot of criticism."

"I'll believe it when I see it. I owe DeLane a lot. I hope he has changed, not like J. W. though. I believe that whatever J. W. Moss does is purely opportunistic for business reasons, not out of any moral impulse."

"We owe J. W. a lot. You don't know all he's done to help me with the farm and the land sales."

"I just hope he isn't cheating us out of everything we ever had."

"J. W. is a good businessman, but he's as honest as any man I've ever known, and he takes care of us. You have to give him a lot of credit. I think he ran for years on co'colas and moon pies and chewing tobacco, cut off in strips with that little pearl handled knife of Charlie's that I gave him."

"Maybe I don't understand the customs and mores of racial relations in Morganville, Mother. Maybe I don't want to. It doesn't cut a lot of ice with me that someone like J. W. Moss is a little more tolerant than some other local bigots."

"Well Byron, you'd better start wanting to understand if you're planning to accept Kermit's offer to be the high school principal."

"Explain it to me then. Tell me what I'm missing."

"Oh, son. I wouldn't dare talk to you. It'ud be like me telling boys down at the Ford place how to fix cars. You've got all that technical education about poetry and literature. I'd feel stupid trying to explain how things are down here to you. You'd make me feel dumb; you know you would."

Byron had no reply. She was right. Whenever she'd discussed modern poetry with him, he'd regarded her ideas as naïve. He stood and walked over and sat on the back of his mother's chair and put his arm around her. She was trembling and beginning to tear. He kissed her on the forehead, but even that gesture seemed premeditated and condescending, not a spontaneous act of affection.

"I will try to understand. I know it's important if I'm going to be an effective principal."

Later Byron realized how prophetic his own words would be, but at this moment he was still unaware of their import.

Despite longing to see DeLane again and being reminded of their youthful escapades as he revisited familiar scenes in Morganville, Byron was paralyzed by his ambivalence, fearing that they would not be able to reconnect as adults; and so he never drove up to the used car lot to see DeLane and never called him on the phone; but on the last week of June, DeLane appeared late one afternoon at the front door of his mother's apartment.

"I'uz real sorry to hear Miss Reen's got cancer." DeLane sounded like an embarrassed little boy who didn't know what to say in an awkward situation, as if cancer was a pesky summer cold to which his mother was susceptible, as if these words were in the middle of a conversation that had been continued from earlier in the day, not his first words of greeting after fifteen years.

"Come in, DeLane. It's really good to see you. You're looking good."

DeLane wore khaki pants and loafers and a light green nylon shirt that showed his white undervest beneath it. He had a belly, a beer gut; but his arms were still as strong and muscled as ever, even though his face was older.

"I got fat."

"The extra weight looks good on you. You've got the chest and shoulders to hold it up." It was true. Byron thought that he would have looked like a crooked beanpole that swallowed a watermelon with a gut like DeLane's, so he had to diet and watch his weight.

They laughed. "I reckin. How's Miss Reen?"

"She's responding well to the treatment, but it tires her out. She's taking a nap right now. I know she'd like to see you, but I wouldn't want to wake her up."

"That's awright. Tell her I asted after her, but I was really comin' to see you anyways. Hit's been a long time." There was judgment without accusation in DeLane's words and tone of voice.

"Lots of years." There was a tone of apology and regret in Byron's words, and he turned away from the piercing green light in DeLane's eyes.

"They say yo're movin' back down here. You ever git married?"

"No, I was dating someone very seriously and thinking about asking her to marry me. I guess I need to decide what I'm going to do."

"Yeah. I know all about that. I done been married and divorced twict."

"You have any children?"

"Nope. Lucky, I reckin, not to have no young'uns to put up with after being married twict, not to mention t'other women I've had . . . That's a whole 'nother story." DeLane's voice trailed off, and Byron wondered what the other story involved.

"I hear you run a car lot up on the highway. What else have you been doing since you came back? I guess Morganville is pretty dull after living in the big city."

"I go fishin' right much up at Canebrake Beach. Hit's still on yo're property, I guess. I got me a fishin' boat and trailer. That's part of what I come down here fer. To ast you to go out fishin' with me. It'ud be good fer you. You ourghten to set up here in this here house all the time, seben days a week, like J. W. says you do. I know you got to take kere of Miss Reen, but you need to git out and do some'um else sometimes." DeLane had rehearsed his long speech of invitation; and Byron was humbled, thrilled, and yet still ambivalent about accepting his offer, lest he lose the precious memories of their youth, if they couldn't relate to one another now.

"I don't know. I haven't done any fishing in a long, long time. You have my permission to fish up there any time you want to though."

"They Lord God Awmighty. I didn't come down here to ast yer permission. I ain't about to ast Byron Ashford's permission fer fishin' at Canebrake Beach!" DeLane grinned; and if Byron had looked only at his eyes as they shot out green sparks, it might have been twenty years ago.

"Well, all right. I'll go with you sometime."

"Sometime's about like nevermind, Byron. Lookee here. Nex' Wednesday afternoon I'll call you up. I shut down the car lot ever' Wednesday afternoon and most usually go fishin'. If Miss Reen don't have no doctor's appointment and you feel like you can leave her, yo're a'goin' with me, and I ain't acceptin' no excuses."

"Okay." Byron spoke like a little boy, once again letting DeLane set the agenda, as if they were playing a game of tag.

"That's better. I'll come by fer you right after dinner." DeLane put his hand on Byron's shoulder and then reached around to the center of his back and rubbed the lump with his palm and squeezed it with his fingers. No one had touched Byron that way for fifteen years, since the summer Mother had sold the big house and moved into town, since the afternoon that DeLane had given him the map to the whorehouse in Rome. No woman nor any other man had ever touched him that way, not Mother, not Sally, not even Hattie long ago.

On Wednesday well before Noon Byron heard a car horn honking outside and from the window saw DeLane in a white and red Pontiac convertible pulling an aluminum fishing boat behind it. As Byron opened the front door DeLane was halfway up the front walk. "Go git on some old clothes. We're a'goin' fishin'."

"I haven't had any lunch yet. Have you already eaten?"

"I got our dinner and the bait and a fishin' rod fer you out in the car. All you need to do is go in and put on some fishin' clothes."

At Canebrake Beach the water was clear down deep into the liquid blackness, rather than muddy on the surface. DeLane knew how to tie and bait the lines, and he enjoyed refreshing Byron's memory.

"Reckin' you didn't larn much about fishin' up at college." DeLane was as agile as he'd been twenty years ago.

At first they caught only a few small bream and took them off their hooks and tossed them back to the river; but within about an hour Byron snagged a big bass and struggled with it until he could feel the sweat pouring down from his head and over his shoulders and around the lump on his back, which felt like a rock in the middle of the stream. Then the perspiration flowed down his spine, as the river flows down its bed, until it emptied between his buttocks. He winced when he took the hook out of the fish's mouth, and DeLane cackled at him. The quest not the kill had brought him pleasure, and he'd felt a quiet joy in floating down the river in DeLane's presence, but he found an even greater thrill in DeLane's admiration at his triumph. Byron didn't mind the thin cold fish blood on his hands. It seemed more like vegetable juice than the warm thick blood of forest animals, which he could never bring himself to kill. DeLane had brought two six packs of beer and potato chips and sardines and catsup, but he'd forgotten to pick up crackers or bread for the sardines, and they ate them on big sugar cookies with the catsup poured on top. It tasted terrible, and DeLane was truly embarrassed by his omission as the host on Byron's first adult outing with him. Byron teased him unmercifully and felt once again closer to him than he'd ever felt to any other man.

Few fish were caught during the rest of the afternoon. Byron's bass was the great event of the outing. As the sun dropped low into the sky, they tied up the boat and lay back on some cushions, smoking cigarettes and talking until dusk, as they'd talked together on the big flat gray rock by the creek as boys. DeLane told Byron about his customers at the used car lot and the way he sold them pieces of junk when they acted like know-it-alls and wouldn't pay attention to his advice or recommendations. The life of a high school English teacher seemed drab in comparison to the adventures of a used car lot owner. Perhaps two boys who had swum naked at Canebrake Beach and who returned as men couldn't hide behind the artificial rankings of society. Here the world began anew each day and ended with dusk; and as Byron and DeLane had once swum and fished as boys at Canebrake Beach, they now talked again like two souls that had been born afresh together that very morning without any distinctions of inequality between them.

By the time they pulled the boat in and loaded it onto the trailer, they'd made plans to build a boathouse together at Canebrake Beach; and Byron had decided that he would probably accept Kermit Stoner's offer to become Principal of Morganville High School for the year while he took care of his mother.

The next day Byron stopped by Kermit Stoner's office to discuss accepting the position of Principal of Morganville High School. "I still don't know if it's such a good idea. I have a lot of respect for how you've integrated the school system here. What if I go and mess it all up?"

"You're not gonna do that."

"I'm not real sure I can carry out things your way. I have my own way of doing things."

"Now I don't go fooling around with the principal's business, Byron. You run the school your way, and I'll not interfere. If you need help, then you holler. I've never claimed to be an educator; I'm just a country politician. We have a tradition down here of having a superintendent who handles the political side and a principal who takes care of the academic side. It's worked pretty good over the years."

"You told me all the teachers are hired and set for the year."

"Yep. That's the one good thing George took care of before he up and left. I leave the hiring and firing pretty much up to the principal, though the by-laws say I've got to approve. Same way as the board leaves selecting the principals up to me, though they've got to approve 'em by the law. Sometimes I'll do the firing to take the heat off the principal. I'll cover your ass if you don't go and bloody mine, you know what I mean?"

Byron grinned. He liked Kermit Stoner. His father had talked about running for county school superintendent several times, partly because he was a close friend of Kermit's and would have enjoyed working with him as a colleague in the other system in Davis County. "The sixty-four thousand dollar question, what's happening with the integration of the school? I know it hasn't been easy for you."

"Lord knows things have been rough at times. Integration was a pure mess. The colored people didn't want it any more than we did. The colored children even staged a protest march to keep us from closing down Carver School, and we had to let most of the colored teachers go. They didn't have college degrees for the most part. We didn't lose but a very few white children though. We kept over ninety percent of our students. We haven't had any bad trouble. It's gone right smooth. We're pretty lucky, I guess."

"You do have a few black teachers in the high school, don't you?"

"Five teachers and the basketball coach. Coach Harris. Let me tell you, we're damned lucky to have him. He's very popular with the white children and the teachers, too, even with most of the parents."

"What are the racial problems like in the school now?"

"Don't have any. Never have had any. We had a few fights between the colored boys and the white boys the first year and a few between colored girls and white girls—a couple of those were dillies, let me tell you. Well, we expelled both parties for two weeks, with no excuses allowed. And that ended that, right quick. You may have some fights among the whites and some among the coloreds, but you can be right sure you won't have much trouble between the races. They keep to themselves real good now. Course, lots more Negroes drop out of high school than used to. That's a shame, I 'spose; but it's not our fault. Our people tried to tell the federal government what'ud happen. In separate schools you can have a little different standards, but in the same school you've got to treat everybody the same, not make any allowances or exceptions. You've been a school man long enough to know that. It's hard for them; but if they've got what it takes, they'll catch up. I can remember the people coming to me over the years, a long time before there was any integration, and asking for special favors for their little Susie or to let their little Johnny graduate without passing algebra—you'd be surprised at the people if I told you their names. Well, it might make it easier for you right then, but you'll sho'ly catch hell within a few years if you let such a thing get started. Treat everybody the same, I say. The Negroes'll just have to make it like everybody else."

"How are people in town, outside the school, taking integration?"

"They've accepted it fine. Just fine. Mind you, it doesn't hurt to have colored boys playing football and on the basketball team making the winning points. Do you realize we won all but one of our home football games last year? First time I remember that happening since I became superintendent. That helps a lot, especially with the kind of people that were most adamantly opposed." Kermit Stoner paused and looked over the top of his square gold-framed tri-focal spectacles. "Well? What you going to do, Byron?"

Byron paused for a moment, aware of his own hesitation. "I've never been associated with public education before, as I said when you first asked me. Are you sure you want me?"

"Sure I do. Public education's gotten to be a pure pain in the butt. Integration's the biggest headache—plumb wore me out after I was already too old to cope with it—but that's not the half of it. Used to, you could run your school system and talk with the mayor and council and read the state requirements and benefits, if you were a reasonably intelligent man; but now, Lordy me, you got forty federal departments and forty state departments to fool with, and you got to be a Philadelphia lawyer to run a little one horse school system like Morganville. You're a whole lot better off in a private school like the one where you taught, but I'll be damned if I'm gonna give in to the Davis Christian type schools that are popping up all over the South. That's no education at all."

"It makes my blood boil that they use *Christian* to stand for *segregation* at those so-called schools." Byron had been uncomfortable with some of Kermit's diatribes about the integration process, and he was grateful to find a note of common outrage.

Kermit slapped his knee. "You and me are gonna get along fine, Byron. Mixing education and politics is bad enough; but when you stir religion into it, it's a shit house stew."

"What would be your first piece of advice for me as I get started?"

"Just be tough. Don't let the students or the teachers either one get by with anything at the beginning. Let 'em know who's boss. First trouble you have, you expel everybody connected with it for two weeks and don't give in to their parents' pleading; and you won't have any more trouble. The colored people of this town don't want any trouble. They're not gonna cause any problems."

"I hope you're right."

"They won't let you whip children any more. It's a wonder any of 'em ever graduate. We get 'em through school the best way we can, and they're mostly good kids. I can remember some years back when the graduating class was real outstanding. We've had some classes here that stayed close for years and years, stayed friends all their lives. It's sorta sad now though. You can't have the dances after the basketball games and the school picnics together any more. The senior class used to take a trip together every year, even up to Washington, D. C. You remember that?"

"Yes sir, I do."

"They'll never be able to do that again."

And Byron resolved that if he could do anything about it they would have the chance to do those things again, at least some of those things. He believed he had just found a reason to serve as Principal of Morganville High School this year, beyond the very real need for money to support himself and pay his mother's medical bills and have something to occupy his time.

"MAYBE I SHOULD BUY a fishing car from you for driving out to the farm."

"There ain't no call fer that. I al'ays got some ol' heaps traded in settin' up here 'at you kin use whenever you like. Most of 'em not good fer nothin' except bein' junked anyways."

"That Studebaker over there looks like the one you drove around in when I was finishing high school, the last time I saw you before you moved back here."

"Hit's the same ol' car. I never could git rid of hit. Sentimental, I reckin. It'ud be a good 'un fer us to use for fishin' and takin' up to the river. Let's us see how it drives, fer old times' sake."

Before they left the car lot, DeLane showed Byron where he hid a key to a shed with a box on the back of a shelf containing ignition keys for the older cars, in case Byron ever wanted to borrow one for driving to the farm by himself. They'd decided to put a barbed-wire fence along the highway with a metal gate on the road that led down to Canebrake Beach. They would put another fence and gate closer to the boathouse, but Byron would hire someone that DeLane recommended to build the boathouse itself. It was a project beyond the scope of their skills and available time, even under DeLane's direction.

DeLane made the holes with a posthole digger, and Byron carried the posts from the pile where they'd been dumped when they were delivered earlier in the week and packed the dirt around them. DeLane stripped off his shirt and tee shirt, and Byron was surprised how much hair had grown over DeLane's chest and belly that had once been smooth; but Byron didn't take off his shirt, even when it was wet with perspiration. It was still not enough like being with DeLane in the old days that he could expose his back. When the posts were in place, they strung the barbed -wire. DeLane had brought a wire stretcher—he'd brought all the necessary tools—and held the barbed-wire in place while Byron attached it to the posts with a staple gun. They both worked hard and became exhausted, although DeLane did the most difficult and strenuous jobs, as he'd done them when they were boys; but the two men were needed in order to accomplish the tasks; and Byron was one of the essential men, together with DeLane. After the fence was finished, Byron felt a sense of pride, as if it were some great achievement of his life. He told himself that what he was feeling was an adolescent emotion, so that he never expressed it in words until DeLane pronounced his judgment. "It's a purty good fence."

"Best fence that ever was." They laughed at Byron's exaggeration, and their eyes glanced at each other to confess it was not really a joke to either of them, and then they laughed again.

"I'll tell you what I'm a'gonna go do. I'm a'goin' swimmin'."

"I didn't bring my bathing suit."

"That shore never stopped you before."

"We were just boys then—over twenty years ago."

"Suit yerself."

DeLane sat on the grass beside the river to take off his shoes. Then he stripped the sweaty clothes from his skin with his back to Byron. He never even glanced around but leapt into the water like a fierce beast chasing some invisible prey beneath the surface and began to swim violently with a primitive, untutored butterfly stroke. He never looked at Byron, although he may have seen him out of the corner of his eye as he twisted and turned in the current, and he certainly never cajoled Byron to come in with him; but after a few minutes Byron gingerly, modestly took off his clothes and slipped into the water quickly and quietly like a lizard, as if he were trying to avoid being noticed by the flailing monster.

Byron felt more like a boy than a man in the current. The cold water soaked his public hair and filled it out like a sponge—a sensation impossible to experience when wearing a bathing suit. Then he sank below the surface. The damp cold touched his back and sent chills of pain through his body. He no longer felt any discomfort; he was absorbed, and he and the river became one. He thought how good it would be to stay beneath the water forever and never think of the troubles of the world again. Floating on his back and looking up through the summer branches thick and full with leaves, he tried to imagine the sky as a dark patchwork green and the flecks of blue as tiny flowers on bare limbs and twigs.

Byron thought that he'd stayed in the water only a short time; but when he got out, his sweaty clothes had already dried. He stood naked on the bank watching DeLane swim until the drops of water evaporated from his skin. For him it seemed more modest to stand in the nude facing forward rather than backward, so that his back was not visible; but with DeLane he didn't need to hide either his penis or his back, because neither mattered to DeLane now any more than they'd mattered a quarter of a century ago when they were boys. DeLane was the only person in the world who had always accepted him completely as he was. DeLane swam more calmly now and bobbed up and down breaking the surface of the water and submerging himself over and over again. They had neither spoken nor touched nor even looked at each other in the river, but the deep black water of the current below the surface seemed to have bound their souls again as they had been united years ago as life-long friends at Canebrake Beach when DeLane had saved his life, as if it were a sacrament renewed from the time of first communion.

After DeLane dried himself and dressed, they lay on the grass on the bank beyond the sand smoking cigarettes and talking as the sun set. "What do you suppose the school board would say if they'd seen their new principal skinny dipping?"

"J. W. he wouldn't give a shit."

"J. W.'s on the school board?"

"Yep. I bet the kids'ud get a kick out of it though." DeLane laughed. "They might like you a whole lots more. Leastways they'ud know you was human."

Byron took out his wallet and removed a small piece of folded paper from an interior pocket and handed it to DeLane. "Know what this is?"

DeLane unfolded the ancient creases gently as if it were a precious medieval document. "Hit's my writin'. I don't recollect when I writ it though. You got me." He handed it back to Byron.

"It's the map you drew for me to the whorehouse in Rome."

"When was that?"

"The first time I ever rode in your Studebaker . . . or any Studebaker for that matter."

"Did you git laid?"

"The first time for that, too. You were gonna call me the next day to be sure I went through with it."

"They Lord God Awmighty, what a mem'ry. I bet I never called you up."

"You never did."

"So, you got your first piece of pussy, huh? But yo're still holdin' a grudge about me not callin' you up? Yo're worser 'an my second wife."

Byron laughed. "No grudge. I just never had a chance to thank you. I doubt I would have had the courage to be with a woman or almost get engaged, if it wasn't for you."

"Shit, Byron . . ." DeLane turned away and bit his lip. "You would've got somebody to help show you . . . or found out by yerself. I didn't do nothin' special."

"Yes, you did. You saved my life when I was a little boy right here, and . . . well . . . showed me how to be a grown up man."

"Shit, Byron. You al'ays did tell things and make me say things nobody else did. You're the goodest friend I ever had in this here world, and that's God's honest truth." Now Byron turned away. He didn't want DeLane to see the tears in his eyes. "I'll tell you something I never told nobody before, not even my wives. I wanted a kid more 'an I ever wanted anything in this whole world, and I never could have one. I talk about not wantin' no youn'uns all the time, but that's just a big show. Hit's a lie is what hit is."

"Are you sure?"

"Oh, yeah. I al'ays figured some'um was wrong with my wife, but then my second wife she knew about them things. She'd gone to college like you and made me go see a doctor, a urologist. Well, he give me a stack of *Playboys* an' told me to jerk off in a jar, and they come back an' told me I was shootin' blanks. Ain't that a howdy-do, with me fuckin' half the women in Atlanter. I never let on to my wife. I told her the doctor said ever'thing was just fine." DeLane's pain was so apparent in his eyes that Byron couldn't look into his face.

"I'm sorry."

"Anyways, I can sleep around much as I want to without worryin' about bein' brought up on no paternity charges." His bravado dropped once again. "Alvin he's got two boys and a girl. J. W. and Sylvia's got a son. Hit don't seem fair."

"Life isn't very fair sometimes."

DeLane finished his eighth beer of the afternoon; Byron had drunk four out of the twelve that they'd brought with them for the work project. "You don't look down on me 'cause I shoot blanks, do you, Byron? I ain't never let on to nobody a'tall that I can't have no child'urn."

"God no, DeLane. You've always stood for what it means to be a man to me, and you still do. I'm really sorry you can't have children of your own, but you're still the best man I ever knew. You always will be."

"Don't never tell nobody what I said to you. You was always my goodest friend, Byron. I loved you more 'an even my own brothers growin' up and that goes for now, too." DeLane put his arm around Byron's shoulder and rubbed the lump on Byron's back with his palm and squeezed it with his fingers.

Then Byron put his arm on DeLane's shoulder. He'd never dared to reciprocate before, after DeLane had stroked and squeezed his back; but now he felt the right, the need, even the obligation to touch DeLane after the confession of his secret, after the revelation of his pain. As soon as Byron's fingers touched DeLane's flesh, he giggled; and Byron remembered DeLane's extreme ticklishness. In all his frequent, almost daily, memories of DeLane over the last two decades, he had never thought once about how ticklish DeLane had been. Now DeLane was giggling like a prepubescent child. Giggling hadn't seemed to fit Byron's image of DeLane, even as a boy; and now his ticklishness seemed to mar the pride that Byron had felt from the secret DeLane had shared with him and made it seem almost comical and absurd.

THE SUN WAS SETTING when Byron unloaded the last box from his car. He paused on the marble steps of the school building to look at the sky. Despite the July heat he enjoyed feeling the gray silk twilight and the black velvet night of a Georgia summer. Barn swallows, that the local people called chimney sweeps, gathered like a fog of gnats around the roof of the Baptist Church on the hill across town. Music and lamplight rolled out of the small nearby homes like bright toys spilling from a child's chest onto the street.

The plaster walls inside the school were remarkably cool under his searching palm as he sought a light switch; but even in the darkness, waves of heat from the rooms that been closed up for weeks folded out into the night air. Schools had no character at night, because they were empty of human presence and voices, in the same way they lost their personalities in the summer.

An overhead fluorescent fixture buzzed and provided the only light in the principal's office, and Byron failed to find a place to plug in a lamp for his desk. The sight of his office in the artificial light startled him, as if the bare walls cried out at being unexpectedly disturbed. He wondered how anyone ever wrote or read at the desk, nevertheless worked on a dissertation—perhaps none of his predecessors ever had.

When he crawled under the desk to see if there was a floor outlet, he hit his back on the drawer edge. As it throbbed with pain, he remembered, as he often did when he the lump on his back ached, the sad and unhappy times in his life. It was a bad omen for beginning his work as the Principal of Morganville High School.

"Hi-yo, can I help you some way?"

Byron hadn't heard anyone enter the building, and he was so startled and frightened by the voice that he hit his back again as he crawled out from under the desk. This time the pain was so severe that combined with his alarm at the intrusion he could hardly speak. The tall muscular black man was wearing a white tee shirt and shorts. If he hadn't been wearing shorts Byron might not have identified him. Black men rarely wore shorts. He must be an athlete . . . a coach. Then Byron recognized the face that he'd studied, whose black eyes had held him motionless as he'd looked through the faculty personnel files yesterday.

"Coach Harris?"

"Yep. You know me?"

"I was looking at your photograph in the faculty files yesterday, but I almost didn't recognize you . . . in the dark."

Earl Harris had the face of a chieftain, the face a boy dreams about confronting in a heroic battle and then converting to friendship in a pact of brotherhood. Just as Byron had experienced the impression of having met Coach Harris, when he'd stared at his photograph yesterday, he once again wondered if they'd met somewhere in the past.

"What are you doing over here at this time of night?"

"I could ask you the same question."

"Checking on equipment at the gym. I couldn't remember what was left from last year that I'd packed up, and it got to bothering me, so I came over. I saw the lights on over here in the office, and I wondered if something was wrong. What were you trying to do?"

"Sorry. I'm Byron Ashford, the new principal." The pain had abated enough for him to extend his hand. He wondered if Coach Harris had thought he was a burglar or a vandal.

"I guessed that." Earl Harris stepped forward and paused before he carefully and deliberately accepted Byron's handshake, as if the gesture had to be pondered and considered, as if it meant something besides the polite empty ritual when men first meet. Then his face shifted to a grin, as if a solemn portrait in a gallery suddenly smiled or a statue came to life. "Can I help you?"

"Oh, no thanks. Unless you know where there's an outlet in this room. That's what I was crawling around on the floor looking for—to plug my desk lamp in."

"It's behind the bookcase. I only know 'cause I helped your predecessor move out." The word *predecessor* from his lips seemed only slightly more unexpected than his swift movement to the bookcase, which he grasped by each end and shifted to the side of the room with outstretched arms that looked like an eagle preparing to fly—all in one sweeping motion. "You'll need an extension cord to tape it down on the floor. I'll pick one up for you and move the bookcase back over in the morning when I come to the gym."

"That's kind of you, but I couldn't ask . . ."

"You didn't ask me. I volunteered. You'll have a lot to take kere of getting settled in." Something in *kere* didn't fit his articulate speech patterns,
as if the word had been borrowed from someone else, from long ago, from
another time and place. "Is there anything else I can help you with tonight?"

"Not tonight. Thanks though. I'm really glad to meet you." Byron smiled;
but Earl Harris didn't smile again, as if he counted his smiles and parceled
them out stingily. Byron restrained himself from stretching out his hand
again, like a flustered little boy in the presence of a celebrity.

"Well, goodnight, then. I'll be getting on home. My wife will be wondering what became of me." Byron smiled again at his pleasantry, but the coach's
face remained solemn even as he spoke the words in a teasing tone of voice.

As Earl Harris turned away he rose on his tiptoes, and a flood of word-
less memory washed over Byron leaving only mysterious feelings in its wake
without any names or times or any relation to things that could be identified. Perhaps it was Rudolf Nureyev, in the ballet that Byron had driven
from Tennessee to Atlanta to see, even though Earl Harris was much taller
and bigger and probably stronger than Nureyev; but he'd never seen any
other man walk and move with such grace except for the Russian dancer.

Byron heard the click and thud of the heavy front door with the big
spring at the top that looked like a deformed elbow. He realized that he
was once again alone in the building, but he felt far more alone than he'd
been before the coach's visit. Thunder rumbled faintly with the glow of
heat lightning, not frightening or startling. As it began to rain, huge drops
splashed as they hit the pavement; and when Byron opened the window
several drops fell on his cheeks almost like tears that might have come from
his own eyes. He didn't know if his feeling of sadness arose because he'd
lost something that he couldn't remember or because he might never attain
something that he couldn't imagine.


EVEN DOWNTOWN ON MAIN Street white people greeted Earl as "Coach
Harris" and referred to him as "Coach Harris" in the private conversations
that conveyed their sincere regard and respect, unlike the artificial "Mister"
that they grudgingly addressed in recent years to black leaders in town
with a suppressed smirk, while they used other titles and names in private.

Only a few years ago they'd used given first names in public, together with a variety of derogatory epithets ranging downward from "boy" to "the Harris Nigger"; but as a good basketball coach Earl Harris occupied a unique position that made him immune to the injured pride of the present or the racial vanity of the past.

Byron once asked Earl Harris to call him "Byron", but Earl soon reverted to "Mr. Ashford" and had never suggested a reciprocal "Earl". Then Byron considered calling Earl "Mr. Harris", in order to accord him honest esteem and respect; but it seemed contrived; and so he conformed to the prevailing cultural arrangement and called him "Coach Harris" along with everyone else.

In the halls of the high school between classes Earl was the only teacher who touched the students and was touched by them, always appropriately, always affectionately, with a hand on a shoulder or occasionally an arm around a neck or a pat on the back; it was the coach's legacy, still available to be claimed, even by a black man; but the students and the coach never tousled each other's hair as former coaches and students and coaches had done. Earl's coarse, black, curly hair was too different and thus too private, avoided almost like a touch below the waist, as if it were taboo.

Byron knew that Earl had a free period when he saw him pick up his mail and the school announcement sheet from the teachers' cubicles in the foyer of the principal's office. "Come on in, Coach Harris, and have a cup of coffee with me."

"I'm not a coffee drinker, Mr. Ashford. Thanks, anyway."

"I got some tea bags, if you'd prefer . . ." Tea seemed such an unlikely beverage for "the Coach" that Byron teased him in the macho-mocking tones that people often used in addressing him, but Byron wouldn't suggest a Coke; he wouldn't press too hard, too eagerly for conversation or for friendship. Earl Harris would think of bringing a Coke himself if he wanted to continue another old ritual, the privileged hanging-out of the principal and the coach for a few minutes of casual banter every morning, something that no other teacher was privy to.

"Tea's good." He grinned, one of his rare grins that raised his cheeks like polished round knots of wood and showed the full length of his front teeth like a squirrel's.

"Have you never drunk coffee? Or did you quit it for health reasons . . . as an athlete?"

"When I was a boy delivering papers up in De-troit, I went by this café every morning; and this white waitress would ask me if I wanted some black mud and smirk, and I swore I never would drink it again." The smile turned into a scowl so angry and severe that it frightened Byron; but the back of Earl's eyes seemed to open, as if an inner shield had been removed. "It seems sorta silly, I guess."

"I didn't know you grew up in Detroit."

"My mother was sick a lot, and my relatives took care of me most of the time up there." Earl rose up on his toes, like a dancer, as if it were a teasing question, asking Byron to supply the answer; but when his heels touched the floor again, the smile and the scowl had both hardened into a wooden mask, and the shields behind his eyes closed so that nothing more would be revealed. Once again Byron thought that if he could recall something that was lost or misplaced in his memory, Earl Harris might share more of himself in true friendship. The rest of their conversation was stiff and formal. The curtain into Earl's soul had been drawn open only for a brief moment, like a tantalizing promise.

When he came into the foyer the next morning, Coach Harris brought an opened bottle of Coca-cola, sipped a quarter of the way from the top so that he wouldn't seem presumptuous about chatting with the principal. He paused waiting to be invited into Byron's office, testing to see if Byron's invitation had been genuine. So the ritual was re-established between the principal and the coach, and almost every morning Byron and Earl spent ten or fifteen minutes sipping a cup of coffee and a Coke. Occasionally Earl would request a cup of tea, as if spurring Byron again to some unremembered commitment of the mind or the will, but they always talked formally and addressed each other carefully as "Mr. Ashford" and "Coach Harris". Whenever Earl left the office and at other times during the day when Byron saw him rise to his toes and prance down the hall with the silver coach's whistle bobbing on the silver chain between the muscles of his chest like a small clapper in a big bell, he would feel the pangs of constipated memory like bowel pain between his ears trying to remember.

THE AUTUMN TEMPERATURES MADE fishing at the river less than ideal, but Canebrake Beach was the only place that Byron felt an equal partnership with DeLane, and so they continued their weekly fishing ritual until the weather became really cold. Because Byron needed to stay in his office at the high school on weekdays, they put out their trotlines early on Saturday mornings before DeLane opened his car lot and checked their catch on Sunday afternoons.

When DeLane called one Friday afternoon to say that a trailer of cars was coming in very early on Saturday morning and he couldn't leave to put out the trotlines, Byron thought it would be best to wait until the following weekend; but DeLane said the weather was too good now to miss a week—there weren't that many weeks of fishing left in the year—and that Byron could put them out by himself so that they could go back together on Sunday afternoon to haul them in. Byron didn't want to go out on the river alone. DeLane asked if he couldn't find some teacher to help him the next morning. It was issued as a command, and Byron realized that their fishing on the river had become as important to DeLane as it was to him. A few minutes later Coach Harris arrived in the foyer to check his cubicle, and Byron asked him if he would like to put out some trotlines and share the catch if the fish were biting.

"Sure. I'd be glad to. How long do you think we'll be?"

"It shouldn't take us more than a hour or so after we get the boat into the water."

IN THE BRIGHT SUNLIGHT on the river Earl's skin seemed lighter, the color of the copper statuary of white segregationist politicians on Georgia courthouse lawns, where their faces were memorialized for posterity in the colors and hues that they'd ranted against during their lifetimes.

When the lines tangled, Earl leaned over the side of the boat. His shirt pulled up above the band of his undershorts, and two streaks of brown flesh moved beside the row of vertebrae, as the muscles declared what it was to be an athlete even more expressively than the movements of his arms and legs during ball games. He couldn't reach the tangles, so he took off his shirt and shoes and slipped his pants down and rolled over the side of the boat. He dived beneath the water and broke back through the surface several times before he found the snarl.

As Earl continued to try to loosen the knot, Byron felt guilty and helpless and awkward remaining in the boat. He leaned over the side of the boat in an attempt to help, but he couldn't do much from inside the boat, so he tied the boat to the low limb of a tree that stretched close to them. Then he took off his shoes and pants, but he left on his tee shirt that covered his back and slipped into the brown and gold liquid beside Earl like a creature that lives in a hole on the bank, causing hardly a ripple in the surface of the water. Then he went below the water and once again became a part of the river.

Byron's mind and soul seemed to float in the stream, and the outer enclosure of his body was dissolved. He lost the separate body that made him different and separate from every other living thing in the world when only air surrounded them. The river and the rocks and the trees and Earl Harris and Byron Ashford belonged to one world, to one instant in time. Perhaps individual men could never come together through their wills, because of love and justice, but must discover that they already belong to some common world of which they had been members long, long before.

The line was finally untangled. Since the boat had been tied up to the tree and they were already wet, they decided to swim, as Byron and DeLane often did after they'd finished putting out the line; but Byron and Earl swam in their underclothes, not skinny dipping like little boys, not like swimming with DeLane.

Earl swam briskly, moving across the river with powerful strokes, while Byron paddled and waded and floated. Earl swam back toward Byron to rest, breathing heavily from his exertion. "It really is a beautiful place, like you said."

"It's the kind of afternoon that you wish would go on forever. The river can be dangerous though. I almost drowned here as a little boy. I wouldn't get into the water even now with just anyone, unless he was a strong swimmer."

"Doesn't seem possible that such a peaceful looking, beautiful place could be so dangerous. Looks are deceiving, I guess."

Earl pulled himself up into the boat with a powerful thrust and held the tree limb with one hand to steady the boat and extended his other hand to help Byron out of the water. Earl was glistening in the sun, and streams of water danced across his skin like serpents of fire. Even his majestically carved wooden face became all quickened flesh. As Byron arched himself awkwardly over the side of the boat, Earl's hand reached across Byron and his long fingers lightly touched the lump on his back, as if exploring it curiously, fearfully; and suddenly Byron remembered how Early had touched him long years ago.

Byron spoke as if he were a ventriloquist's puppet in Hattie's lap, almost echoing her exact voice from those long years past. "You be Early! You were born too soon, such a little bitty thing that no one knew if you'd live, so they named you Early; but you grew up into this big, fine man."

"That's so." Earl was laughing. Byron had never heard him laugh before. His body shook, and he shook the boat, and the river and trees seemed to shake with primordial laughter, as if it were the first laughter to be heard in Creation. Even when he stopped laughing, Earl continued to smile, and his face and body seemed as transparent as a freshly washed windowpane, so that Byron could look down through it into his soul, where nothing was hidden, no question could remain unanswered.

"Of course. You grew up in Detroit and came to visit Hattie that summer. Why didn't you tell me who you were?"

"I guess I really wanted you to remember on your own."

"Did you ever see Elmo and Tancy again, after they left the farm and moved to Michigan."

"They were more like my immediate family than just cousins. Mama was sick so much of the time."

"You never did come to Canebrake Beach the summer you visited the farm, did you?"

"Nope, but I remember you talking about it. I can remember you telling me it was the prettiest place in the world."

"I still think so."

"Elmo used to talk a lot about Canebrake Beach, too, 'specially after he moved to De-troit."

"Elmo was one of my favorite people growing up as a child."

"You didn't treat him very well though. Elmo meant a whole lot to me.

I hope I can look after my daughters as good as he looked after me."

Byron could think of no appropriate response. He might have said, "I was just a little boy" or "It was what people had to do in those times" or "I'm not responsible for what my father did"; but he tried instead to change the subject. "Why did you move down here to Georgia?"

"I started working right out of high school and going to night school. I played basketball, and some coach from down South saw me and offered me a scholarship to finish college in Georgia. I really thought you'd remember me. I guess one black man's face looks just like another one to you." Earl's voice teased. It wasn't the dry voice of bitterness that he often used when he talked about white people, but the accusation was evident.

Byron felt an anger rising in his throat that he couldn't understand. "That's not true. I did remember. I remember playing with you. I remember seeing your high school picture clipped out of a newspaper that Hattie showed me when you won a big race. I just couldn't put them together, the little boy I played with and the teenage athlete and who you are now. I don't know why I couldn't remember. I'm sorry . . ."

"That's all right. I'm just foolin' with you." But the windows into Earl's soul had closed, and Byron and Earl were once again as separated and enclosed within themselves on the drive back to town as they'd been on the drive up, as if the afternoon at the river binding them as friends had never happened but was only dreamed or read in a book or somehow forgotten and misplaced in their memories.

ON THE WAY TO the river on Sunday afternoon DeLane asked Byron who had helped him get the trotlines strung and baited.

"Earl Harris came up with me. I promised him part of what we catch. He really knows what he's doing. The line got all snarled, and I never would have gotten it untangled by myself."

"The Nigger coach? You took the Nigger coach up here with you?"

"I wish you wouldn't use that word. I know you don't mean anything by it, and people used to say *Nigger* all the time, but it's insulting now."

"The hell you say. I'll talk however I want to. I don't know why you want to go fishin' no ways. You don't never eat nothin' we catch. Well, you can give him a mess of fish. Niggers loves catfish."

DeLane was sullen for the first hour on the river. Byron wondered if he remembered Earl Harris and how he'd hit his head with a rock as a little boy, although Byron always believed that DeLane hadn't meant to hurt him, that it had been an accident. When DeLane and Byron checked the lines, they found a larger than usual catch. "Reckin yer Nigger buddy'll git hisself a good mess o' fish. You think yo're right smart takin' that Nigger out in my boat."

"Are you really that upset that I took the coach up here?" Byron eyed DeLane to see if he detected any trace of memory about Earl from the past.

"I don't like that you done it to show me up, same as you showin' off yer Nigger lovin' ways fer ever'body to see over at the schoolhouse."

Byron didn't reply for several minutes. "Just what is it that bothers you so much, that I try to treat black people as I treat everyone else?"

"Hit makes you feel a whole lot smarter 'an other folks who still tries to keep their place above Niggers, don't it?"

"No, I just try to do what I think is right."

"Makes you feel better 'an them then."

"Are you really that sore that I took Earl Harris fishing because he's black?"

DeLane spat out some tobacco juice. "Naw. I don't give a kere *that* you done hit. Whites and coloreds been fishin' together on this here river since people first come acrost the Canebrake. I just kere for *why* you done hit and *how* you done hit."

"Without telling you or asking your permission?"

"Tellin' me *after*. Proud as a peacock and all swole up and about to bust. I done heerd about hit anyways before you tol' me, from some of the boys in town."

"If it ever happens again, I'll try to let you know before we come up. I know it's your boat. It belongs to you." Byron thought, *As Canebrake Beach and the boathouse belong to me*, but stopped himself from saying it out loud.

"I don't give a shit who you take out on the river, but hit galls me whenever you come back at me tellin' me how I'uz suppose to talk, so goldurned highfalutin'."

Secretly Byron enjoyed believing that DeLane was jealous of Earl and wanted to claim his exclusive friendship. Byron thought that DeLane didn't really harbor any ill will toward black people. He merely talked the way he'd been taught as a child, and he didn't have the advantage of knowing black people as equals and participating in the Civil Rights Movement as Byron had experienced them during his college years and thereafter.

ON MONDAY WHEN EARL Harris came for his morning break with Byron in the principal's office, his expression reminded Byron of the flickering images of an old silent movie, where the characters are seen and then hidden in darkness in blinking succession. During the instants when the shutter was open, Byron thought he saw a vulnerability and hurt in Earl, even a kind of fear and panic, until he closed himself off with a façade of bravery and strength.

"What's the matter, Earl?"

"Lordy, is it that obvious?"

"You just look like something's wrong."

"It's not all that much. Last night some hoodlums threw garbage and tin cans all over my yard and up on the porch and yelled a lot of . . . Nigger things. It upset Annette and the girls right bad."

"Earl! Did you call the police?"

"No. I don't want that. I don't want to make a whole lot over it. Not now. Not yet."

"Do you have any idea who they were?"

"That's what bothers me so much. I thought things were going along right good. I thought . . . people liked me here. Well, you never know."

"Everyone does like you. Everyone who's spoken to me does. The kids practically worship you. You can't make too much out of one isolated incident, no matter how ugly."

"That's what I don't want, why I didn't want to call the po-lice and have it publicized."

"I'm glad you told me. You have to promise to tell me if anything like this ever happens again. We'll hope it was just a crazy isolated incident. But I want you to know I'll do everything in my power to help you and protect you and stand by you, if . . ." Byron could feel his throat tightening with emotion and the pitch of his voice rising and crackling. "Earl, you have to promise me . . ."

"I will. Thanks, Byron. It means a lot to me." Earl patted Byron on his shoulder, but he didn't touch his back again, and several minutes passed before Byron realized that they'd called each other Earl and Byron for the first time. Although there had been a tension between them as they recalled their childhood friendship, perhaps that memory allowed them to be Byron and Earl once again to each other. Or perhaps they were bonded, despite their lingering uneasiness with each other, just by being together in the river at Canebrake Beach.

THE FIRST WEDNESDAY OF October was as warm as an August day by Noon, in spite of the chilly dawn. *An apple picking day*, Byron thought; and he remembered how the Moss boys had shed their shirts and flung off their shoes to climb the trees in the orchard that his great-grandfather had planted and how they'd handed down baskets of fruit as fleshy as the boys' arms and shoulders.

Julie Hemphill, one of the new teachers straight out of college, tapped lightly on a glass pane of his office door. The sheer floral fabric of her dress alternately blew away from her body, like a curtain blowing against a window in an autumn breeze, then it clung to her as she walked. Watching Julie made such an apple picking day at least barely tolerable for the male students, as well as the male teachers, who endured the fetid, body-odored shade of the school but ached to run and stretch and yawn in the sun of the long summer's last day. If she noticed the leering, even by the principal, she did a good job of pretending to be oblivious.

"Come in, Miss Hemphill."

"Mr. Ashford, I want to discuss a problem concerning a student with you, if you have a few minutes."

"Of course. Please sit down."

She sat on the edge of the chair and thrust her breasts out toward him as if she were offering them as autumn fruit for him to gather. "It's about Mose Harbin."

"Morganville High's football star?"

"He's failing my class in junior English."

"How badly?"

"Very badly indeed. He doesn't even have a fifty average."

"There's not much hope of his passing, I take it, even if we arranged for a tutor and put the fear of God in him."

"I don't see how. I talked with one of the older teachers . . ." She flushed and glanced self-consciously away from Byron and by doing so confirmed her accusation that he was also older and long past the sweet flesh of autumn's apple pickers, even if he'd ever possessed a secret tender body of beauty beneath the clothes that swaddled the lump on his back. ". . . I mean one of the teachers who has been here for several years, and she said that the principal can rule on it. Allow him to play, I mean. I hate to do this to the team and Coach Lyons and Coach Harris. I hate it for Mose, too. He's such a sweet boy."

"Have you talked to the coaches about the matter?"

"No sir. I wanted to come to you first."

"That was good judgment. I'm new around here, too; and I don't know all the rules yet . . . especially those that aren't written down anywhere." He smiled, trying to establish some link, some shared communion with her. "Let me talk to a few people and see what I can do. In the meantime, I'd appreciate it if you didn't mention it to anyone else. Your discretion would be valuable. I'll take care of it and let you know what I decide to do and what action we may need to take by the end of the week, first of next week at the latest.

"What about Mose Harbin?"

"What about him?" Earl munched a peanut butter and cheese cracker and tried to corral a crumb from his lower lip with his tongue and held out the packet to offer one to Byron and spoke simultaneously. "What do you want to know about him?"

"What kind of a boy is he?"

"He's the best natural athlete I've ever coached. You've seen him on the football field. I've never known a high school kid who could move like that."

"I'm no big football fan, as you know; but I never saw *anybody* move like that except for Earl Harris and Rudolf Nureyev." Byron couldn't help smiling and pursing his lips to see if Earl knew who Nureyev was and what he would do with the comparison.

Earl laughed loudly and raised his middle finger, and Byron felt himself blush and cursed himself for letting Earl win the joust. Earl laughed more loudly still.

"What kind of a student is he? Is he a good kid? He's flunking English, and I've got to decide whether to take him off the football team."

"You mean is he a dumb Nigger? What would you do if he was a white boy?" Earl's anger often erupted without warning like an inner fire that was released in a sudden volcanic blast and could just as quickly recede again back deep inside him, leaving an apparent calm on the surface.

"I hope I would make the same decision whether it was a white boy or a black boy. Maybe I'd give him a little extra benefit because he's black, and maybe that's racist, too; but that's how it would probably come down."

"Sorry. It ain't your fault." Earl finished the last cracker and dusted his hands and crumpled the cellophane and tossed it overhand, dramatically, across the desk beside Byron into the trash basket. "He's a good boy. He's got soul. He's got spirit. He's got a heart as big as Santa Claus. He's honest, as far as I can tell; I'd trust him with just about anything."

"Maybe if we can get him some really good tutoring he can come back next semester for your basketball team."

"Don't kid yourself. As quick as you take him off the football team, he'll quit school. He's sixteen. He'll never play basketball one way or the other. God knows I wish I could coach that boy again next year. You can give him permission to play out the fall semester if you want to; but when first semester grades are in, there's no exception to the rule unless Julie Hemphill just passes him, and she's not gonna do that. I know her type. I'd really hate it for Coach Lyons, too. I'm just the assistant coach for football; but this is probably the only shot he'll ever have at the state championship. I'm a lot younger than Coach Lyons. I might have another chance at state with basketball, if I live long enough."

"Can you answer one more question without getting completely steamed? Is he intelligent or is he just not capable of learning?"

"Listen, Mose understands complicated football plays in his head as good as he moves those hips to keep from getting tackled. He's no dumb Nigger." This time he said it softly, almost as a whisper and added almost like a prayer of imprecation, "He just never had a chance. He's too far behind to ever catch up."

"Maybe I can help him."

"Forget it. This time next year he'll be digging the man's ditches or trucking the man's freight—for the rest of his life. You might as well write him off."

"I don't write people off. I have to try to do something."

"Suit yourself. White liberal aristocrats always were turned on by lost causes more than anything else. If you get your jollies . . ."

"Fuck you, Earl Harris." It was easier for Byron to curse with his words than with his fingers; but if Earl's bird had been good-natured with a resentful seed, Byron's voice was serious and damning with a seed of good will, even of charity buried somewhere deep inside. Earl tried to smile; but it was as if the mechanism that pulled his cheeks up into little round balls had failed, and he brushed a tear back but feigned something in his eye and immediately pulled the upper lid over the lower one.

"Yep. I'm glad you want to try, even if it won't do any real good."

BYRON WANTED TO TALK with Kermit Stoner before he made a final decision about Mose Harbin; and when he called, Kermit said that he would stop by the school during the afternoon. "I like to drop in from time to time. It gives a little reality to all the paper shuffling over here at the superintendent's office."

Byron pored over the records of Mose Harbin's grades from the past five or six years before Kermit arrived, just before classes were dismissed for the day.

He explained the situation to Kermit without using any names—not Mose's, not even Julie's, not Earl's or Coach Lyons's—but he suspected that Kermit knew who all the people involved were. Kermit kept up with all the events at the school in an uncanny way.

"Well, let me say first off that this is your decision, and I'll back you up one hundred percent no matter what you decide to do. It's completely up to you. There's precedent both ways. Sometimes the principal has pulled a boy off the team. Sometimes he's let him go on and play till the end of the semester. I think it all depends on the boy. I know I'm always talking about treating everybody equal; but you can't really do that in this case, because there're not two boys on God's green earth that are exactly alike. Every one of 'em is different. Have you talked to the boy yet?"

"No, sir. I plan to do that before I make my final decision."

"That's a good idea. Let me give you one piece of advice though. Don't talk to Coach Lyons till after you've made up your mind. It sho'ly wouldn't do any good, and it'd just get everybody all riled up."

Byron chuckled. "That's good advice." He was glad that he'd consulted Kermit Stoner, who had wandered over to the window and was watching the last students and first teachers leaving for the day. He massaged his bald pate with his fingertips in a deliberate quizzical, almost boyish manner. "Byron, who is that girl getting into her car out there?"

Byron stood and glanced over Kermit's shoulder out the window. "That's Julie Hemphill. She's a new teacher." He wondered if Kermit was harboring the same lustful feelings that had occupied his thoughts along with the other males in the school throughout the day and also wondered if Kermit Stoner already knew that she was one of the main characters in the story he'd just related.

MOSE HARBIN LOOKED DOWN at his lap during much of the time that Byron talked to him, but whenever he looked up his eyes focused on Byron's face and never shifted or glanced away or wavered. As a connoisseur of the beauty of bodies and faces, Byron rated Mose as the most handsome boy in the school, perhaps the most handsome man in town except for Earl Harris. *A young DeLane* was the highest accolade Byron's mind could frame. Mose's skin was very dark; but his body seemed infinitely malleable, like some exquisitely smooth resin that could be twisted and bent under the pressure of a great inner strength but that would always revert to its perfect shape when relaxed. Yet, as perfectly formed and lithe as his body was, his face was even more compelling. Earl's angry epithet, *dumb Nigger*, seemed almost paradoxically silly when looking at Mose. If any face ever embodied intelligence, it was Mose's.

"I'm considering letting you finish the football season, playing to the end of the semester; but unless you pass your work you won't be able to go out for spring practice or play basketball."

"Thank you, sir."

"Will you work really hard with a tutor, if I get one set up for you?"

"Yes, sir."

"Will you promise to stay in school, through the spring, if I let you finish playing football?" Byron knew as soon as he'd said it that he'd pushed Mose too far, asked too much, and put himself and the boy in an untenable position and forced him to lie.

Mose looked into Byron's face without answering for a long time, his black eyes piercing as if they were rays of negative light. Then he dropped his head and confounded Byron's predictions. "I can't promise that, sir."

"I've been studying your grades, and I think I may have figured out what's the matter." Byron took a large card from the center of his desk. "Read this for me, Mose."

The stumbling, occasionally mispronounced little words and desperate attempts to sound out syllables of longer words were pathetic, but Mose didn't bow his head. He kept on trying futilely until Byron stopped him. Byron thought that he would have hated any man who had humiliated him in such a way. "You can't read, can you, Mose."

"No, sir. Not much. Not very good." Again Mose looked steadily into Byron's face and wouldn't deflect his eyes, but there was no hatred reflected in them.

"Do you want to learn how to read?"

"Yes, sir; but maybe I'm too dumb."

*Look down, please look down*, Byron thought; *turn away your eyes.*

"You're not too dumb. And don't be ashamed. We're the ones that ought to be ashamed, all of us who haven't taught you what you should know. We've failed you, Mose. Don't you ever be ashamed. I promise you that I'll teach you how to read. If you'll stay in school, I promise you on my word of honor that at least you'll learn how to read."

Finally Mose did look down, but he didn't reach up to staunch the streams of tears that ran down his dark cheeks like silver veins until they all merged at the cleft of his chin and dripped off onto his hands which were folded serenely on his lap. Byron was reminded of the statues of the young Buddha and felt almost reverent and self-consciously guilty at continuing to watch him. Mose opened his mouth, as if he would speak; but no sound came out. Byron thought he would allow him to sit there until he was composed, and he stayed for a long time; but before Byron told him to leave, he rose and wiped his face discreetly with great poise and deliberation and started toward the door, as though he would accept responsibility for his own fate and would allow no man to command his coming and going. At the door, with his back to Byron, Mose said, "Thank you, sir. I promise I'll try my very best."

As OCTOBER MOVED ALONG, the nights chilled, and the warm days that had been enjoyed at the beginning of the month frosted like panes of glass that were spotted with opaque grey ice until they were completely covered without any transparent spot. Even the juiciest apples were now cold and crisp, unlike their warm and juicy flesh on the mellow days when the first ripe fruit was gathered from the tree.

Ever since Morganville High School was integrated, a black homecoming king and queen had alternated each year with a white homecoming king and queen. If artificial arrangements needed to be imposed, surely a more felicitous plan could have been arranged—two couples each year, for instance, one white and one black, Byron thought; but he couldn't easily alter a Morganville tradition, albeit less than five years old. The students, however, felt no such obligation to conform to the nonsensical practice and rebelled, electing Mose Harbin as the homecoming king and the fairest blonde cheerleader as the homecoming queen. Byron was both amused and delighted by their impetuousness; but he was also perplexed about how to handle the public relations, not to mention the public ceremonies, with both tact and dignity.

As usual when confronted with a conundrum, he dillied and he dallied, not so much cogitating on it as pushing it to the side of his mind in the vain hope that it might simply fall off the edge and go away; and as sometimes happened, when he was lucky, it was taken out of his hands, so that he didn't have to deal with it. The students themselves came up with the solution to their own dilemma. Rather than face their more prejudiced peers and more contentious elders, they decided that both the king and the queen should choose an escort.

Homecoming night brought perfect football weather. Byron was almost giddy with an unexplainable joy and pride at halftime. Mose had played an excellent first half; and even though he looked slightly disheveled in the middle of the field standing beside Judy, Byron's favorite student secretary, whom Mose had chosen as his date. As he held his helmet in one hand and her hand in the other, he was as close to a romantic, medieval knight in his padded uniform as any teenage Georgia boy ever gets to be. Judy wore a white lacy dress, tea length, the girls called this style, with a full puffy shirt and carried a single rose; and with her large Afro and black skin was surely a fittingly lovely lady for this errant, chivalrous hero.

The official queen was less regal. Her blue satin dress was both too long and too tight for striding easily across a football field. Silence had accompanied Mose and Judy's walk down the fifty yard line, either out of respect or contempt; but teasing yells and whistles responded to the queen's stumbles. Her companion rushed her rather than supporting her and seemed to enjoy her plight in a slightly sadistic way, although ostensibly trying to cover their awkwardness with humor.

During the second half Mose made two spectacular touchdowns, and his photograph appeared the next morning on the front page of the sports section of *The Atlanta Constitution*. Byron didn't regret helping him to achieve the one moment of glory that every man deserves for some flashing, shimmering instant of his life. Byron hoped there would be more such victories for Mose; but even if his promises and pledge failed and Mose never learned to read, he had received the honor and adulation of his peers, which every true and self-effacing hero deserves at least once in his life. "Ah, verray, parfit, gentil knight," Byron mutter as he folded the paper, so that he could continue to look at the photograph as he ate his breakfast cereal and toast.

Byron was still gazing at the photograph of Mose in the newspaper, transfixed as if he were praying before an icon, when Earl's telephone call interrupted his meditation. "Sorry to bother you on a Saturday morning."

"That's okay. What's up?"

"We had another incident last night. It was right bad. Annette's all upset."

"What happened?"

"They drove by throwing rocks. One of 'em busted out my front window. My girls were near 'bout hysterical."

"Earl, this is serious. It's time to call the police."

"Not yet. We've got to avoid getting into a situation with black people and white people taking sides in town."

"But you've got to protect yourself. You've got to consider your family's safety first."

"I don't want to go to the po-lice with it yet, but I had to talk to somebody. I apologize for calling you, but . . ."

"What can I do for you, Earl? Just tell me. I want to help."

"Nothing. Just listen, and don't tell anybody else yet. I know you won't go talking all over town. Just don't tell anybody at all. I had to tell somebody though."

"I still think you're making a big mistake in not going to the police now."

"There is one thing. I caught a glimpse of a car this time. It was an old model, green, I think. I couldn't read the license plate. You could sorta ask around who drives an old car like that, without people suspecting anything, like if I asked."

Byron was shaving before he thought of their fishing car, the old pea green Studebaker. He knew that DeLane had told several people, as he'd told him, where the keys to the old cars were hung from a shelf in the shed behind the lot. Byron wondered if some lowlife friend of DeLane's might have taken the car out of the lot and driven it to Earl's house for the terrible night of vandalism.

MORGANVILLE HAD NEVER BEEN affluent enough to hire a regular secretary for the principal's office; and the tradition of students acting as secretaries was an old and hallowed honor, which the best commerce students still regarded seriously. Every time Byron walked out into the reception area, he imagined Sylvia Jones (Moss) there as a high school girl. It would seem natural somehow to see her sitting stiffly in the typist's chair with her eyes on a steno book and her fingers on the typewriter keys. Sylvia had moved from the principal's office directly to Ovid Phillips' insurance office when she graduated from high school. She'd broken the speed record in both shorthand dictation and typing, and she still held the record for shorthand, but Judy Evans had overtaken Sylvia's record in the number of words typed correctly per minute.

Byron tried to save all his correspondence for Judy because she did accurate, beautiful work. She was his second period secretary, and he enjoyed her lively face and chatter. The other two girls typed abominably and spelled worse. They rarely spoke without giggling, except for the days when he reprimanded them; and then they remained sullen with only "yes sir" and "no sir" replies.

"Mr. Ashford, can I talk to you for a minute?" Judy had grown the largest Afro at Morganville High School. She was tiny, and her pretty frail face danced constantly inside her huge frame of hair.

"Sure, Judy, please sit down."

"Oh, no, sir. I'll just stand up. It won't take that long. I don't know whether to say this or not. You've been real nice though, and I thought maybe you'd understand."

"Go ahead, Judy. Blurt it out."

"Mr. Ashford, why can't we have a prom and a sports banquet? Just tell me what's wrong with having the prom and banquet again. They used to have them every year; and if you took a poll of all the students, I bet nine out of ten would vote for having them again."

"It's something to be considered. Homecoming king and queen worked out without any big problems, even if the students did pull a fast one on me in the election. But you looked mighty pretty at the game with Mose."

"Thank you, sir; but please don't go changing the subject on me." Her eyes sparkled, and she smiled, so that he wouldn't accuse her of impudence or anger. "That's what the white folks sometimes do on us, you know, sir, try to change the subject. Just give me one good reason why we can't have the prom and banquet again."

"The only reason I've heard not to have them is that it might put you students in danger." Byron remembered the recent incidents at Earl Harris's home; but even if he were not pledged to silence, he couldn't have talked about them with Judy. "If someone outside the school, someone that we have no control over, hurt one of you because he didn't like an integrated dance, it would be terrible. I have the responsibility for thinking about that kind of possibility."

"Oh, Mr. Ashford, we can take care of ourselves. I'll bet you that if somebody tried to hurt one of us, all the boys, black and white, would jump him. I don't think any trouble-maker has the courage to take on our whole football team."

"Judy, you know how unpleasant things can get." Byron recalled that she'd been one of the first black students to integrate the junior high school under the old freedom of choice plan.

"Yes sir, I know. When the four of us first went to junior high. Silence." She passed a level hand through the air. Judy gestured with every sentence. "Nobody said one solitary word to us. Then they started saying bad things. Honest, Mr. Ashford, I didn't even know what those bad words meant. I don't know where those sweet little white girls learned them. I've always been a fighter. If somebody jumps on a girl all by herself, I don't care what she's done, I get in there and help her fight them. In grammar school I was always like that. My mama talked and talked with to me about staying out of fights, but that's just the way I am. Well. When I got to that junior high school and was sitting in the classroom, they let go with twenty-five spit balls right on the back of my head, and the teacher didn't say one solitary word. And paper clips shot with rubber bands. Ouwee! I can still feel the sting. Well. I raised up real slow and mean and turned around, and I looked into those twenty-five faces, and then I eased myself back down. And I said to myself, Judy, girl, you just as well decide to take it or leave out 'a here, because this is one time you just can't fight nobody, 'cause you can't fight everybody. It was that way all year long. I had to be real meek and solemn, and I hated it, 'cause that's not the way I am. It's a wonder I don't have permanent bumps on my head from all those flying missiles."

"You see why I'm reluctant about arousing the people that are prejudiced. Of all people you should know that once violence starts a lot of people can get hurt."

"But things are different now, Mr. Ashford. They're not great, but they're a whole lot better. We can have the prom and banquet all right now. I know we can."

"I give you my word, Judy; I'll think about it. I won't promise anything, but I'll think about it and talk with Mr. Stoner and the school board about it and try to work something out."

"Thank you, sir. I know you can convince them. I just know it will work out okay."

"You may be putting too much confidence in me. Don't get your hopes built up too much."

Judy smiled and turned to leave, but at the door she thought of something else, as people often seemed to do at the point of leaving Byron's office. She turned back toward him. "I want to thank you for all you're doing for Mose, too. It means a whole lot. It's important."

"Yes, it is." *More important than the symbols and events that mark integration*, Byron thought, more important than proms and banquets, because what he was doing with Mose involved saving a man's life; and suddenly Byron remembered how DeLane Moss had saved his life from the cold dark water of the river at Canebrake Beach many years ago.

AFTER SPENDING THANKSGIVING DAY with his mother Byron had intended to leave on Friday for a visit with Sally in Tennessee, but he decided that his old car needed new brake pads. When the phone rang, he expected that the mechanic was calling to tell him that everything was ready; but Earl's voice responded, "Elmo and Tancy came down to visit for Thanksgiving, and they wondered if you'd wanted to come over and see them."

"I'd like to very much, but my car's in the shop."

"Hey, I'll pick you up, if you don't mind ridin' in my old heap. We're having car trouble, too; and Annette's car is at the garage. I knew you were leaving, and I think Elmo and Tancy are planning to come by to see your mother while you're in Tennessee."

Earl's old rattletrap car had once been a dark green. Now it was flaked and flecked. The seats were covered in gray scratchy wood material like Irene Ashford's pre-war Plymouth, except that these seats lacked the bulging ridges;

but Byron felt the gray wood with his palms, rubbing them back and forth beside his legs as he'd done thousands of times when he was a little boy, as if they were a furry animal. It almost seemed that a towel should have been spread for him to sit on, as his mother would have done, so that his skin wouldn't be chafed, if he were wearing shorts; but unlike the pristine condition of Irene Ashford's car long ago, the gray material that had once been attached to the ceiling of Earl's car flapped as they drove.

"I'm sorry about this old trap. I usually swap out with Annette when I ask anybody to ride with me." Earl's wife kept their new gold-colored car during the week.

"It's fine. I like it. It reminds me of my mother's car when I was a little boy."

"I never asked any white man to ride in this old heap before." He glanced slyly at Byron. "You got to lay out your best for the white folks."

As soon as Earl opened the door at his home for them to step inside, Byron felt a hand on his shoulder and whirled around as he heard the whisper, "Mista Byron." After all these years his first impulse was still to repond, "I told you never to call me Mister." But Elmo laid a finger over his pursed lips as if he'd heard Byron's thoughts.

"Elmo! It's so good to see you. When did you get to town?"

"Couple a' days back, but Tancy she's still wore out."

"That's Tancy?" Her skin was paler than his mother's; and he remembered protesting long ago, "Hattie's not a Negro; she's whiter than you are." Tancy was dozing in a chair. "Gosh, it's been over twenty-five years since I've seen her. I wouldn't have recognized her." The skinny, frail girl was now a plump, middle-aged woman with the inevitable sags and budges that years without proper care cause in a woman's body.

"Near 'bout that since you seed me, too."

"You don't ever change." Byron believed that Elmo didn't change, because he needed to believe that one thing in his world never changed. Elmo was wearing khaki pants and a khaki shirt with the sleeves rolled up to his elbows and the top two or three buttons open at the neck, revealing his undershirt beneath. Byron had never seen him except in overalls before. Although he looked a little older, his body was still as strong and sinewy as ever; but his face had changed in a way beyond aging—the last traces of fear and panic and anger were missing.

"Who is it?" Tancy stirred in the chair. As soon as she opened her eyes Byron knew that it was Tancy who hadn't changed. Fear and panic, if not anger, still flickered across her face.

"Tancy, you know this here boy? You believe this here's Byron? Little ol' Byron done growed up."

"I know him. How are you, Byron? It's good to see you." Her pitch and cadence had been influenced by a quarter century of city voices, while Elmo's voice and speech were exactly the same as they'd been on the farm.

"I'm fine. I didn't know you at first . . . with your eyes closed."

Tancy smiled but still spoke very little.

Elmo broke the silence. "I bet you done fo'get how I cook fo' you. You use' ta love my cookin'." Byron thought that he probably often spoke when Tancy was quiet.

"I never will forget that. The supper you always cooked the night after Dad sold the cotton was the best food I ever ate. Better than Thanksgiving dinner, then or now, I bet." Then Byron remembered refusing to go to Hattie's house after the harvest during Elmo's last year at the farm because they were black and DeLane made fun of his eating supper there.

Elmo winked at Byron. "Nex' time we come visit Earl I'll fix you a mess a bacon and taters in the fireplace. Show him you' gran'baby's picture, Tancy."

"He don't care to see no photos."

"Yes, I do. I want to see your family, all of them. Do you have some recent pictures of your daughters?"

Tancy smiled and took her billfold out of her purse. The baby looked like all babies to Byron. Their daughters were attractive.

"They're pretty girls. Byron remembered seeing their pictures at a much younger age when he'd visited Hattie. "I saw their pictures at Hattie's a long time ago."

"Me and Tancy's thinkin' 'bout movin' back down here to Morganville, Mista Byron. They say they fix a job up fo' me in the plant down at Doraville till I get my retirement."

"That's a long way to drive every day."

"When I left out'a the farm, I never did figure me ever havin' a car, bein' able to drive myself up to Atlanta. Can you figure that?"

*Please don't call me Mister*, Byron thought; but he said, "It'll be good to have you closer by again." And he heard his mother's phrases and tone in his voice.

"Tell Miss Reen I'm a'comin' to see her by Sunday. Long time, long, long time I ain't seed Miss Reen, and I still think a whole lots of her."

On their drive back to Irene Ashford's apartment, Byron reminisced about their lives long ago on the farm. "I wish things could be as simple and happy as they were then."

"No, you don't. 'Cause nobody wants the poverty and the suffering that go along with that kind of simplicity. That kind of life didn't treat Elmo and Tancy so good."

"I didn't mean that . . . I know people suffered a lot under segregation, and the Ashford farm was no utopia, but I do think there was a lot of love between my family and Hattie's family and a lot of good things came out of our relationship."

"All the Niggers were treated real good on yo'a Daddy's plantation, huh?"

Byron wanted to change the subject and escape Earl's sudden wrath that broke without warning like an unanticipated storm. "I know you saw a different side of things when you visited during that summer. I remember when you got hurt. Do you still hold that against my father?" Byron remembered how his father had turned away and said nothing at first, when he looked at Earl's wounds. Byron remembered how he'd been ashamed and angry and afraid and alone, as if no one might help him either or protect him from the bad things in the world. Byron had believed that bad things would always be punished and that his mother and father or other big and powerful people or God would protect him from danger and suffering. Byron's mother had taken Earl to the hospital and hadn't heard his father's reprimanding words to J. W., words that partly restored Byron's belief in the order of the world.

"Not exactly. I don't hate your daddy on account of that; he got your mother to take me the hospital and all, but I hate J. W. Moss for what he did to Elmo and Tancy. And, yep, I guess I blame your daddy for letting him do that to Elmo and Tancy. It's not about what happened to me. Kids will get in fights and all, but what J. W. did . . ." His hatred and anger had so dried his mouth and lips that he couldn't speak any more words, and the sounds from his throat seemed almost like the curse of some malignant demon.

"If I can ever do anything to make it up to Elmo . . . I never understood why they left the farm so suddenly."

"It's sort'a funny. Elmo probably had a better life up in De-troit than he ever would've had in Georgia. He managed to work regular and get a little education. He even bought a house, and their older daughter went to college before she married and had a baby, and their younger daughter just started to college. It wasn't your daddy's intention to do him any good turns, though." Earl wiped his hand across his dry eyes, as if he were weeping.

"Right before Dad died he did whatever J. W. told him to."

"I already told you I don't feel about your Daddy the way I feel about J. W. Moss, but he knew right well that Tancy was Hattie's daughter by her second husband and Elmo her first husband's son by his wife that died before he and Hattie married. He knew they were no blood kin. Maybe he couldn't resist J. W. Moss's determination to get rid of all the Niggers on the place. He said either they had to leave or all the Mosses would pull up and leave. He wouldn't live in a place with families having sex with one another."

Byron felt a chill. He wanted to jump out of Earl's car and run away, to hide and never have to face him again. "I'm sorry. I never knew anything about that."

"Yep, I didn't know what the word *incest* meant until I got to college, but I knew what damn lie it was a long time before that. It's hard to forgive your daddy for that."

Byron hadn't reached out to touch Earl when his head had streamed with blood from the rock that DeLane had flung. Then even his smooth, round little boy's arms and legs had been knotted in tense, painful springs, as his huge athlete's muscular arms were now. Byron's hands and words still couldn't reach out to comfort him, neither then nor now. "I wasn't trying to excuse Dad; but I can't pay for the sins of past generations, not even my own father's. Dad was always too passive. I believe he just gave in to J. W. He didn't ever say those awful things about incest to Elmo, did he?"

"They never told me the sordid details." A strange look crossed Earl's face. Then he smiled, mechanically. "I don't think so, from what they did say." Earl had decided to tell Byron what he wanted to hear. He used the old game that a black man had played with a white man for the past century or more. It was the white man's version of the truth that Byron received, mirrored back, the only version of the truth that a black man had once dared to utter before a white man and now the only version of the truth that a black man bothered to return out of his contempt.

"Maybe Elmo and Tancy did have a better life than they would have had if they'd stayed in Georgia. Their girls are pretty. Elmo and Tancy's girls."

"They're real nice girls. I used to baby sit for them. I guess I sort'a had a crush on Tancy. I guess your daddy and J. W. would call that more incest, too." Earl didn't smile at his absurd exaggeration; it wasn't meant to put Byron at ease. "She's not much older than me, you know; 'though, Lord God, she looks to be over fifty now. She had a real hard life up there, 'specially at first."

"Is Elmo bitter about what happened to him on the farm?"

"I don't think so. Elmo knows how to keep from getting bitter, more than anybody I ever knew. Other people have to do his hating for him. I never did see any man that could keep himself from hating like Elmo. I can't."

Byron thought that Earl was giving him a warning. Then Earl's body slumped, in the same way that the taut frame of the track star he'd once been had relaxed after his jump. Then Byron peered into Earl's soul and saw him as he'd never understood him before, as if little flashes had illuminated dark caverns deep inside him for a few moments. Perhaps Earl would never tell Byron all of who he really was and so would never receive an understanding of who Byron really was.

BYRON RETURNED TO TENNESSEE for a visit with Sally the week after Christmas. He proposed to her, and she agreed to be his wife. Irene Ashford looked twenty years younger as she read the announcement of their wedding in the *Davis County Herald* and smiled at the photograph of Sarah Elizabeth Rutledge. Her frail body, which usually moved slowly as if it might be torn apart like a model fashioned from tissue paper and balsa strips, now became animated and glided across the room. Her eyes twinkled inside the dark circles and wrinkles of her face as she waved the newspaper like a flag of triumph. "I'm so happy for you, son. Now if you'll just give me a grandchild before I die, I'll be the happiest lady in Morganville."

Although Byron's thoughts had been focused on Sally and their wedding plans, he remembered on the last Thursday of the Christmas holiday to talk with Kermit Stoner about a sports banquet and a prom in order to fulfill his promise to Judy Evans. When Byron looked at Kermit, sagging and stooped behind his desk, he wished that he'd waited and chosen a better time to make his case; but he knew there would probably neither be a better time nor even an easier time.

"Why should we go borrowing trouble, Byron? Things have gone real smooth here lately."

"If we don't let the students have some social functions all together that they can take pride in, we're gonna have trouble eventually. I believe it's time to begin some of the activities that had to be left off the past few years."

"I'm against it."

"Yes sir, you're the boss." Byron rose to leave.

"Hold your horses. You determined?"

"I really do believe it's what we should do."

"Well, I'll handle the school board and the mayor and council and the yak-yak from folks in town. But I'm holding you liable for the students. Just make sure there's not any trouble."

"I'll do my best. You'll be glad, Kermit, when it's all over."

"Yes, I probably will, if I live through it."

Five days later, on a Tuesday afternoon, Kermit Stoner had a heart attack. He'd told the school board the night before that a junior-senior prom would be given for Morganville High School this year. He told them. He didn't ask their permission, and he didn't encourage any debate on the matter. At Kermit's request Byron hadn't attended the meeting. Byron went only when he was asked to be there, and he'd been specifically asked not to be there on that Monday night. Kermit remained in intensive care without visitors throughout the week. Byron felt guilty and blamed himself for Kermit's attack. The Presbyterian preachers of his childhood had said that sins of commission were even worse than sins of omission; perhaps he should have ignored his promise to Judy Evans.

In the hospital Kermit appeared gaunt and bloodless. His bald head looked dull, like a lamp bulb that had always been lit but was now dark. "Byron, that junior-senior prom thing isn't responsible for my attack. And above all, you're not responsible for it. Now I want you to get that notion out of your head."

"I didn't have to come over here to know you were going to say that."

"Well, you're gonna have to fight the bastards by yourself now, but they aren't gonna train any heavy ammunition on you with me laid up here in the hospital. They have that much decency. Anyway . . . fretting over it didn't cause this heart attack. I'm getting' too damned old for all this hoohaw."

"You're a great superintendent, and the school system is lucky to have you. As principal, I'm lucky to have you. Damned lucky."

"No such thing." Kermit managed a weak chuckle. "You're pickin' up my bad language. You better watch yourself around the kids. Now you listen to me. Don't argue with anybody. You tell 'em you and I decided there was gonna be a dance, and that's that. You needn't worry about the sports dinner. I didn't even mention that to the board. Just do it; but don't argue with 'em, whatever you do. I'll back you up, if I have to. They won't go against me too much with me sick and all."

"I'll take care of it."

"I know you will."

"Is there anything I can do for you or get you?"

"You might see about bringing me a bottle of bourbon."

"I'll see what I can do."

Byron met Dr. Edwards in the hall. "Would it hurt Kermit Stoner to have a little bourbon in the evenings?"

"It's against hospital regulations to bring liquor inside here," Dr. Edwards growled and squinted at Byron through grizzled brows the way a principal is supposed to look at an errant student.

"I know that . . . , but just hypothetically?"

"Hypothetically speaking, it wouldn't do him any harm. Might even do him some good, but don't you go sneaking a bottle in here."

"I wouldn't think of it. It's good to see you, sir. How's Mrs. Edwards?"

"She's just fine."

"Please give her my best regards." Byron turned and walked away until Dr. Edwards called him.

"Byron."

"Yes sir?"

"Kermit drinks Jim Beam."


BYRON RARELY SAW DeLANE during the winter. DeLane came by Byron's office at the school once, but he seemed even more ill at ease than Byron did at the car lot. DeLane stood on first one foot and then the other and scratched his buttocks like a student that was being reprimanded for misbehaving in class. When Byron had stopped by DeLane's car lot to visit a couple of times, they didn't have much to say to one another after the usual pleasantries and talk about the weather. At the car lot Byron had felt like a fish out of water, as if he'd been thrown up on the bank of the river to flounder and gasp for air and die. Perhaps Canebrake Beach was the only place that they could be equal partners.

Byron was surprised to see DeLane come in the door with J. W. for the sports banquet at the Holiday Inn's restaurant on a chilly night the first week of March. The Holiday Inn was the only venue in Morganville for banquets and wedding rehearsal dinners and the weekly Rotary Club luncheon and bi-weekly Lions Club supper. J. W. and DeLane stopped at the oddly intrusive card table to pay Earl Harris for their tickets. J. W. wore a green leisure suit and a checked, wine colored polyester shirt in honor of the occasion. (It was now as rare for him to appear in public without a dark suit and tie as it had once been for him to be seen wearing anything but denim overalls.) DeLane wore his usual short-sleeved shirt without a jacket. He was the only short-sleeved, unjacketed man or boy in the room. The temperature was well above freezing, so DeLane wouldn't succumb to the quilted jacket, the only article of clothing that varied his attire, summer, winter, spring or fall.

"Ha-yo, Byron." DeLane came directly to speak to him, as he always did, as if Byron represented the most important person at the gathering, the guest of honor to be greeted and acknowledged first, not the most embarrassed, out of place man there, a nerd among the athletes. Byron felt the tense muscles around the lump on his back loosen, like the pod around an acorn about to be released and set free, as DeLane released him from his self-consciousness and allowed him to enter the easy camaraderie of the men. DeLane pulled up a chair to sit beside him at the table. There should be no misfits tonight among the men pretending to be boys and the boys pretending to be men. Everyone, even Byron, was on the team tonight and could even pretend that he'd made the team long ago as they shoved one another's shoulders and put their arms around one another's backs, while their faces glowed, as if they were drunk or filled with some religious ecstasy.

Byron leaned forward to face J. W. on the other side of DeLane at the table. "I really appreciate you coming out tonight. These boys worked hard for their honors."

J. W. nodded in his old, familiar way. "Best football team we've had in near on to ten, twelve years, I reckin."

"Basketball team done pretty good, too. Course they a'done a whole lots better if you'd of let that Harbin boy play. That Nigger coach knows how to git results outa his Nigger boys."

Byron winced at what he thought DeLane had intended as compliments and glanced around to see who had overheard him; but DeLane was as unconcerned about his words as about his bare arms, still as round and muscled and perfectly shaped as those of any teenaged athlete in the room.

After baked chicken and a speech from a guest college coach and jokes about the local coaches, Byron helped to pass out jackets in school colors with red leather sleeves and letters on green wood torsos like costumes for Christmas elves; but the faces in the room grew as serious and solemn as they would at the moment of sacrifice in a Mass. Mose received his jacket last because he was also awarded the trophy for most valuable player on the football team. Everyone seemed to be conscious of his inability to play for the basketball team because of his failing grades in the fall.

Mose paused to thank each of the coaches with a poise and deliberation that the other boys seemed to lack in their adolescent nervousness, as if he'd been carefully trained in aristocratic etiquette by someone like Irene Ashford. "Thank you, Mr. Ashford. None of this would've happened wivout your help." He lifted his trophy slightly, as if offering it to Byron. "I'll keep my promise to try and finish high school."

"And I'll keep my promise to help you do it." Although Byron's words were spoken almost under his breath, they were audible to DeLane and J. W.

The men and boys lingered around the tables after the banquet had ended, as if they hesitated to descend from their raptures back into the mundane world of work and sleep. For a few hours they'd eaten at the table of the gods and even played the roles of gods themselves, but tomorrow they would be ordinary mortals again, some of them less than ordinary in their own self-estimations.

Byron heard plans and invitations being initiated for the team captains to visit the Rotary Club and the Lions Club and the Jaycees. Thus one step would lead to another, and the community might be bound together again with its customary rites and rituals. In a few weeks the black captain of the football team would sit beside the vice president of the Rotary Club for the first time and say, "Yes sir, I think we're gonna have a real good team next year. We may not win every game, but I think we'll win most of 'em," just as the white captain had said during the spring to the vice president of the Rotary Club as far back as anyone could remember. Byron felt a warm glow inside, perhaps like the glow of athletic camaraderie that he'd never personally experienced, at what a good and fine thing he'd done for the sake of race relations in Davis County by reinitiating the sports banquet. He was very proud and pleased with himself.

Finally almost all the boys and most of the men left. Byron no longer saw DeLane among the few who remained to chat with the players that had received awards, but J. W. Moss and Mose Harbin were smiling and talking in a corner of the room. Byron remembered Dad pulling corn with Elmo and talking about harvests and storm warnings in the brotherhood of common sweat. In the fields men didn't seem to distinguish hues of skin, neither in the fields of battle nor in the fields of sport nor in the fields of corn.

Earl Harris zipped the roster of reservations and cash and checks into a bank bag and walked over to Byron. "Could I see you for a minute after everybody leaves?"

"Of course. I think it was a great success, don't you?"

"What?"

"The banquet."

"Oh, sure. Yep. I do."

They sat across from each other at one of the banquet tables that had been cleaned and even stripped of its tablecloth. (The others still had the white cloths over them. Perhaps there had been a spill or a stain on this one.) The First National Bank of Davis County bag was between them, as if they were about to arm wrestle for it. *It would be no contest*, Byron thought, as he imagined Earl's big arms, like DeLane's, but well covered by his conventional grey suit.

"I heard a rumor that I don't like."

"What's that?"

Earl waited as if he expected Byron to know what he was about to say or would make a guess. "I heard that J. W. Moss is planning to put up his name for chairman of the school board."

"That is disturbing."

"What you gonna do about it?"

"Me? What can I do?"

"You can tell him he's not fit to run our schools."

"I don't think that's appropriate. It's not my place."

"Not your place! Hell! You gonna look after the white man's interest, no matter who it is, are you? You don't mind if a black man gets a scrap off the table if it dudn't cost you nothin'." The glow in Earl's face, a clear bright light from the banquet, was burning down into a red coal—not so much angry as contemptuous.

"Earl, we're not talking about race; we're talking about strategy and appropriate roles and boundaries."

"No, we ain't. We're talking about choosing what side you're gonna be on. Your daddy let J. W. Moss run Elmo and Tancy off his place without asking any questions. He never would choose. He just stayed above it all like you're doing now. But you're gonna have to choose. One way or the other, whether you're with the Mosses or with us." Earl's voice had risen, and someone from the restaurant came to the door to see what the ruckus was about.

"It's all right. We're just talking about some school business. We'll be leaving in a few minutes." The hostess left with a suspicious glance back at them.

"Don't you do that! Don't you go apologizing for me. Don't go smoothing things over like your daddy smoothed things over with the Mosses after they busted my head open and then eased Elmo and Tancy off your farm."

"I'm sorry. I didn't mean to do that. I just didn't want to cause any trouble."

"Didn't want to cause any trouble!" Earl's voice was sarcastic, mocking, almost shrill. "It's about time you made a little trouble. Are you for us or against us? Are you gonna help me out here or not? Or are you gonna straddle the fence all your life like your daddy did?"

"I'm with you. I want to help." Byron spoke softly, but for him it was like a sudden oath, a confession from a conversion that had struck him as swiftly as a lightning bolt.

"So, you'll go talk to J. W.?"

Byron felt as if his will and reason had been removed, and he must obey blindly and absolutely like someone who gives himself into the hands of a god to do his bidding and receive divine approval. "If that's what you want me to do, but I have one condition." In his belly Byron felt his free will returning.

"What's that?"

"I'm gonna talk to the police about those incidents at your home, unless you call them. I have a responsibility as the principal of the school."

"I don't want you to do that yet."

Byron held up his hand but withdrew it quickly when he saw that it was quavering. "If I talk to one, I'm gonna talk to the other. I've decided. It's time. I'll be discreet. I'll sound someone out first, Kermit probably, as I usually do, and find out who can be trusted in the police department."

Earl stared at him as if he were trying to see deep inside him, his heart, his motives, his loyalty. Then he smiled; and his face seemed less wooden, once again composed of human flesh. "All right, then, if that's the way you have to do it."

Byron could not have returned Earl's smile if his life had depended on it. He felt very sober, sad, cold, as if he were losing something precious that he loved. All the elated warmth of the banquet had vanished.

As they left the restaurant Byron thought of the time he'd left Morganville after Dad died and had wondered if he would feel different, be different when he came back; and when he'd returned, everything was different, even himself, especially himself. Earl said nothing more as they walked out to the parking lot. They were as silent together as Byron and Dad had been sitting beside each other in the pick-up truck riding over the farm. It was not a comfortable, intimate silence, not then, not now. It was a silence crying out for things that needed to be said; but no one could think of what words to use to say them, not then, not now.

ON MONDAY MORNING BOTH students and teachers seemed to be closed inside themselves, like locked houses with the draperies drawn. By noon, the shades began to go up, and the doors leading inside them were opened, and ideas and smiles and glances passed back and forth between them; but Earl's silence and closedness made Byron uncomfortable, because sometimes Earl stayed locked inside himself for several days. Byron often looked at Earl and talked with him throughout their third period coffee break without any hint about what was going on deep inside him. For all Byron knew, Earl could have been an automaton, moved by wires and computerized parts. It frightened Byron when Earl closed himself off completely, as he'd been afraid when his father had locked him out emotionally.

On Monday afternoons after the students and most of the teachers left, part of Byron's routine involved strolling around the school, in order to see if any window panes had been broken or plumbing in the student rest rooms jammed or obscene graffiti written in the toilet stalls. He found the usual cigarette butts in forbidden corners and what he suspected to be a sprinkling of marijuana beside them. He found a limpid condom and an empty whisky bottle, both, he suspected, planted as pranks over the weekend rather than used on the school premises.

The high school building seemed to have survived another week with only the ordinary wear and tear and with a minimum of light bulbs to be replaced, graffiti to be washed off or painted over, and scars, scratches, and cuts to be ignored until summer repairs and renovations could take place.

Every week he noticed more dents and scrapes and a galloping deterioration and dirtiness. The walls of the halls had been covered with a shiny rubberized tan paint that was supposed to have been washable but had blistered into great pot marks like dried bubblegum collapsed on an open mouth; and the students had peeled off sections of it, leaving jagged pink scars showing beneath the bronze skin.

The students cared for the places that they liked or where they respected the faculty. Miss Gramling's room had no cut desks. It would have been unthinkable to cut the furniture in the beloved, stern old maid's parlor, for that was what her classroom represented, where she'd established her presence. It seemed almost an extension of her, even when she not there. Miss Grambling's room was unlike the anonymous classroom where the new teachers, like Judy Hemphill, taught for a year or two before moving on, where the desks were inscribed with initials and hearts and swastikas.

The gym was also clean and well preserved, and Byron entered it with a reluctant reverence. It was the one place in the school that seemed to be beyond his influence and control, where boys in jock straps and tee shirts might still jump out from between the lockers chanting, "Humpty Dumpty sat on a wall, Humpty Dumpty had a great fall," and bring him to panicked tears. He didn't need to inspect the gym in any case. Earl Harris would assure its order and cleanness; but he forced himself to enter it out of a sense of obsessive, compulsive duty to survey *all* school property, as if it were a requirement for his good character.

Earl poked his head out from the door of his office behind the basketball goal and between the restrooms. Although he looked something like a curious squirrel emerging from a hole in a tree, Byron could see that the morning's darkness and gloom had begun to lift; but something was still troubling him. Earl was always more comfortable on his own turf than he was in the principal's office, just as Byron was more ill at ease in the gym.

"Hello, Coach."

"You looking for me?"

"No, just making my weekly inspection. The gym takes top honors on my clean and shiny list, as usual."

"Thanks. We strive to please." Earl was wearing basketball shorts and a tee shirt, and Byron was aware of his strength and power. Like a priest in his temple Earl inspired an awe greater than Byron had ever felt in a church. "I forgot to ask you this morning if you'd talked to J. W. or contacted the po-lice yet. We had another inci-dent on Friday night. It's gettin' pretty bad. I guess I have to agree with you. It's time to call on the po-lice."

"My God, Earl. After the banquet? They always seem to happen after big school events. No, I'm sorry. I haven't had a chance to do either one. Was it worse than before?"

"About the same. Lots of yelling and trash thrown up in the yard and talk about Niggers."

Earl turned away from him and withdrew back into a silence like Dad's, as if a sudden storm had darkened his soul, as if his spirit had retreated into some hidden cave deep inside his body where no one could follow or even call to it; and Byron seemed to hear the voices of the demonic choir from long ago still echoing in the vast emptiness of the gym, "All the king's horses and all the king's men couldn't put Humpty together again."

"You don't have to worry about talking to the po-lice. I'm gonna do it. This time I got a better look. It was an old Studebaker, like the ones that came out just after the war. And I heard some redneck shouting like a banshee that he was gonna lynch all the Nigger boys on the basketball team and cut out their balls and tie them on his clothesline. I can't let anybody make threats like that about my boys."

"I'll go with you. This is something we need to take care of together on behalf of the whole school. Let's go down there right now." Again Byron wondered if one of DeLane's lowlife friends might have been given access to the tool shed where DeLane hung keys for the old cars on a back shelf, as Byron himself had been given directions for finding the keys and permission for driving the old cars whenever he wanted to.

EARL GAVE THE POLICE chief a detailed account of the events of vandalism at his home; and Byron merely nodded, as if he were only present for moral support or there to assure that a black man would receive a white man's justice by accompanying him before an official in the old customary way that things used to be done. When Earl spoke about the incident on Friday night after the sports banquet, Byron finally joined the conversation. "This is something that affects more than a threat against just one man and his family. This involves the school, too. It jeopardizes the whole community."

"I see, Byron." The police chief gazed at Byron with lowered grizzled brows. He was from the generation of Kermit Stoner and Dr. Edwards and Byron's father, who still thought of him as a boy and would not think of addressing him as Mr. Ashford, according the respect that Byron would usually receive as the high school principal. "Is there anything you can add that might help us with the investigation? Anything that you may know besides what Coach Harris has said?"

Byron remembered his suspicion of the resemblance of the old green Studebaker to the fishing car that he and DeLane drove to Canebrake Beach; but he couldn't bring himself to implicate DeLane, not yet, not until he had more evidence, not until he'd talked with DeLane. Byron owed DeLane at least a direct, personal inquiry.

Byron had ridden to the police department with Earl, who didn't apologize for his old car on this trip; but he needed to finish some work in his office and told Earl that he'd walk back to the school. He wanted to stop at People's Drug Store and pick up the afternoon edition of *The Atlanta Journal*. (He preferred an afternoon newspaper that he could read at leisure after supper; he wasn't a morning person.) He'd inserted his coins and was about to open the little wire cage, when he felt his usual temptation to take two or three newspapers, because it would be a perfect crime. Then he saw J. W. Moss drive up and get out of his big Cadillac sedan.

"Hey, J. W. What're you doing strolling around town in the middle of the afternoon?"

"Reckin I could ast you the same question."

"I was just doing an errand and decided I'd pick up a paper. Have you ever felt the urge to take two or three, even though you have no use for them?"

J. W. chuckled. "Reckin I have. If'n you got caught, it'd be right scandalous fer the principal to be throwed in jail. I'uz jest feelin' a little nauseous and thought I'd come git a powder to settle my stomach."

"I'd been wanting to talk with you since the sports banquet last Friday night."

J. W. turned so pale that Byron thought he might suddenly upchuck on the sidewalk. "Let's go set in my car so as we can talk private."

When they were nestled into the soft leather cushions of J. W.'s Cadillac, J. W. covered his mouth and burped, "'Scuse me. Tell you the truth I think that's what made me sick."

"Something disagree with you at the banquet?"

"Naw. What was it you wanted to tell me?"

"I heard you were planning to run for chairman of the school board. I wondered if that would be a good idea."

"Why's that? Not got enough education."

Byron hesitated. He didn't want appear the old patrician who was insulting the emerging *nouveau riche,* the former landlord putting down the former tenant; and then he decided to ignore his feelings about J. W.'s lack of learning and his personal resentment about J. W.'s treatment of him as a boy and to be frank and candid. "I think some of the teachers might have a problem with your leadership. Especially Coach Harris. I wonder if you even remember that he once visited us on the farm. I didn't, at first. He's Elmo's . . . cousin." Byron felt a flush in his face when he suddenly realized that he didn't even know Elmo's last name.

"I remembered him right off. I've never said nothin' to him about it though. I reckin I ought to. I did make peace with Elmo. A long time ago. I done him and Tancy real bad, and I'm real ashamed of that. He's a real fine man. I tol' him how sorry I was. I reckin you know he's moving back here. I helped him git a loan and give him some help in fixing up a house."

It was almost more information than Byron could process quickly. "Why is it you want to be the chairman of the school board anyway, J. W.?"

"To tell you the truth it's all 'cause of you. I'uz hopin' you'd stay on and be superintendent. I reckin you know Kermit he's fixin' to retire, and I'uz hoping you might take over."

"I'm surprised you'd even want me. I never imagined staying in Morganville. I just came back this year on an emergency basis." Byron was peeved that he'd heard nothing about Kermit Stoner's definite plans to retire and that J. W. Moss was privy to that information.

"Course I'd want you, Byron. You belong here. Yer family goes way back, and yer family and mine has lots between us. You've growed up to be a real good man, and I thought I might he'p you in town if'n you wanted take over the schools."

"I'm flabbergasted, J. W. I don't know what to say. How do you feel about the integration issue?"

"I'm jest fine with that. I feel like we have to move on. I changed a lot in my thinkin' and in my feelin's, too, I reckin. People change. Some of us do." J. W. turned away from Byron and looked out the side window of the car.

"I believe you ought to talk with Coach Harris and tell him some of the things you've told me. You remember how DeLane hit him in the head with a rock and Mother had to take him to the doctor?"

"Yeah, I remember. I'm ashamed of that, too. I'll do hit. I'll go talk to him. Fact is, I'uz afeered the reason you didn't want me heading up the school board was 'cause of DeLane." J. W. belched, and the way his face contorted made Byron wonder if his obvious pain came from something more than a nervous stomach.

BY MID-WEEK THE WEATHER suddenly turned warm, as it often did in Georgia during the early spring. By the weekend the nights might drop close to freezing temperatures again, but Byron used the unusually warm weather as an excuse for talking with DeLane on the pretext of planning what they needed to do to the boat and boathouse before the fishing season. The air-conditioner in DeLane's shack of an office on his car lot imitated the rattle of the old window air-conditioning unit in Byron's school office. They talked about what DeLane needed to do about the boat's motor and what Byron needed to do to the boathouse before they began fishing later in the spring, but somehow Byron suspected that DeLane was aware that there was another reason for his rare visit to the car lot and already knew that he'd talked with the police about the incidents at Earl Harris's home; secrets about police investigations were hard to keep in a small town.

"Have you heard about the incidents at Coach Harris's home over the last few months?"

"The Nigger basketball coach? Yeah, I heered some'um about 'em."

DeLane looked at Byron with narrowed eyes, like a predatory animal looks at its prey. "Nobody's got hurt."

"If you know anything about it, you need to tell the police and put a stop to it, if you can."

"Byron, you ain't got no fuckin' idear what yer talkin' about. Like I said, nobody got hurt."

"Well, people could have gotten hurt, especially this last time, after the sports banquet Friday night. If you know anything about it, you need to tell the police and put a stop to it, if you know who's involved."

"Jest why oughter I do that?"

"Coach Harris saw an old Studebaker like our fishing car roaring away on Friday night. If you know anything about it, you need to tell the police. Does anyone else know about where you hide the keys to the old cars, like I do?" Byron still refused to believe that DeLane could be personally involved in such expressions of racial hatred, but he believed that DeLane might know who was involved.

"Yeah, a few o' the boys knows where I keep the keys out in the shed. Why'd you have to go and talk to the po-lice?"

"I had to."

"Why'uz that? It'uz pro'bly jest some boys havin' a little fun."

"I had to tell them what I knew. It was the right thing to do."

"Yer al'ays off a'doin' some'um 'cause hit's the right thang, ain't you. Looks like you'd want to look after them what loved you and took kere of you all yer life afore takin' other people's sides. You think you can up and make the world over and do anythang you please, anyways you please. You don't seem to know hit's wrong to go out and do some'um'll hurt them that loved you jus' 'cause you think hit's the right thang."

"Sometimes you have to choose between doing something that will hurt the people you care about and doing what's right. It isn't always easy. I hope we can still be fishing partners. I hope we're still friends."

"I al'ays been yer friend, Byron. Yo're the one 'at quit bein' my friend."

"I'll always be your friend, too, DeLane. Nothing will ever change that."

"The hell you say." DeLane glared at Byron. More than anything else Byron wanted DeLane to put his arm around his shoulder, but he knew that would not happen today, and perhaps that would never happen again.

THE SCHOOL YEAR WAS drawing to a close, and the days had become consistently hot by mid-May when Earl asked Byron one Friday morning during their coffee break if he would like to ride out to see Elmo's new house with him that afternoon.

Earl lived in the middle of Morganville across the street from one of the grand old estates that was listed in tourist guides and the registers of historical places and pictured on the back of gasoline company road maps. Housing had never been zoned in *Historic Morganville* along racial lines. The streets there had a high side and a low side. On the high side the columned Greek revival homes were interspersed with humbler but older raised cottages and with modern brick ranch houses. Once slaves had occupied the residences on the low side of the street; and after they were freed, they'd bought or been given their homes and had passed them down to their descendents who continued to work in the grand homes across from them.

Occasionally homes in Morganville that belonged to black men were sold to white men, but rarely were they transferred to the poorer black people from Buzzardtown. The "better class of Negroes" that Kermit Stoner believed came to the city schools had lived for generations on the choice residential streets of Morganville and were as jealous of their status and place as any of the white landholders of the town.

For a few years Earl's home had passed out of his family's hands, but he'd bought back the family homestead when he came to Morganville to coach in the high school. Earl's grandmother, Hattie's mother, had belonged to one of the old aristocratic black families that had been servants to one of the old aristocratic white families; but Elmo, Hattie's first husband's son, had no claim to one of the estates in Morganville, even with educated children and a modest life savings that must have seemed a relative fortune by local standards, all gained up North through tremendous effort and sacrifices and cunning. The way that Kermit Stoner reckoned things, Earl had descended from household slaves and Elmo from field hands; and that was enough explanation for where they lived.

So it was that Elmo and Tancy bought a home outside the city limits of Morganville, in Buzzardtown, an allegorical place laid out into a funnel of misery. The streets ran from Morganville into the edge of Buzzardtown, where the small, neat, white painted houses with trees and lawns and shrubs were indistinguishable from those just inside the city limits (except that they were all occupied by black people and the pavement ended in the middle of a block); but the farther Buzzardtown reached from the city limits, the narrower and more rutted the streets became, the more and more dilapidated and unpainted the houses were, with increasing piles of junk and decreasing vegetation in the yards until at last on the far side away from Morganville there were only eroded foot trails leading past tar paper shacks with tin stove-pipe chimneys and yards littered with muddy rotting paper.

Elmo's house was just across the city limit line. In fact the line ran through his yard which allowed him to receive city water and sewage and garbage service and to vote in city elections but not to send children to the city schools, (a restriction now irrelevant except for the resale value of their house now that Elmo and Tancy's children were grown.) The attractive modern house had been freshly painted, and the cement walk had only recently been poured to intersect with the point where the street pavement ended, at the middle of his lot. Several shrubs were planted beside the front porch with a sweet olive bush beside the front walk.

"Elmo's been working from sunup to sundown fixing up the place while he has a few days leave. He's planted all these bushes himself."

"I can see the results of his labor. It looks really nice."

Elmo came out on the porch to greet them. ""Mista Byron, come on in." Byron winced at the "Mister" especially in front of Earl, but once again hesitated to correct him. Tancy had prepared coffee—tea for Earl—and cake for them.

"I like your new home. It's really nice, and you've done some wonderful things with the yard."

"Hattie taught me good 'bout plants. You 'member her garden? And J. W. he he'p me a lots with the financin' and gettin' ever'thing we need to freshen up the house some."

"He ought to, after what he did to you." The glow in Earl's face was extinguished again, like a lamp being turned off. The picture of Earl and

Tancy walking down the dusty road toward the highway away from the farm flashed into Byron's mind, even though he'd been puzzled by their leaving then and hadn't known the reasons for their exodus; and he blushed for fear that he would embarrass them with the memory, as if they could read his mind now.

"Now, son, you mus'n't hold them grudges. J. W.'s changed for the good. Some folks changes for the good, and some folks changes for the bad, and some folks don't change none a'tall." Byron was afraid that Elmo might be talking about DeLane as well as about J. W.

"I know that J. W. Moss treated you very badly back on the farm." Byron felt himself flush again and hoped that he hadn't been specific enough about what had happened to Elmo and Tancy that they would be hurt by his recent knowledge of J. W.'s accusation against them.

"J. W.'s tried to make it up to us."

"He can never make up for what he did to you." Earl scowled even more grimly.

"Let's us talk 'bout some more happier things. We got to move on. All of us has moved on. Well . . . most of us . . . some of us has moved on. You got to move on, too, Earl."

Byron and Earl sat across the table from Elmo like two boys that had been sent to the principal's office and sat across the desk from Byron for a reprimanding lecture. Long ago when Byron had seen Elmo washing his chest and arms without the loose denim clothing concealing his body, he'd thought that Elmo was the strongest man he'd ever seen. Now Byron thought Elmo was still perhaps the strongest man he'd ever known; but his appraisal didn't involve Elmo's aging body, although its muscular, sinewy shape remained remarkably unchanged.

BY THE FIRST WEEK of May the seats of desks in many schoolrooms were imprinted with the outline of sweaty buttocks after the hot afternoon classes. Vases of scented flowers on the teachers' desks and opened windows inadequately masked the body odors of squirming, discontented adolescents. Couples walked hand in hand along the halls and whispered their vernal secrets only to one another. The girls grinned nervously and stared steadily into everyone's eyes as they met in the hall, and the boys tucked their heads and avoided everyone's eyes. The rate of absenteeism was up, and the number of students who failed to finish their assignments increased.

Except for the annual debate about whether the swimming pool would open, teenagers kept their own counsel and were bored even more quickly than usual by the conversations of their elders. Those who abhorred the thought of black bodies touching white bodies deplored the integration of swimming pools more than any other place, especially during the erotic mornings of spring and the voluptuous afternoons of summer.

Friday afternoon was damp and heavy, and thunder rolled in the distance as the day for the Junior-Senior Prom arrived. Byron was suddenly aware that the incidents of vandalism at Earl Harris's home had all happened immediately following integrated student events, and he remembered his premonition of violence as he picked up his tuxedo from the dry cleaners; but he'd forgotten his fearful foreboding by the time he reached the gymnasium around eight-thirty, after the other chaperons and teachers had come to open the doors an hour earlier, deliberately delaying his arrival so that he wouldn't appear to be anxious and controlling.

His midnight blue tuxedo dated and aged him among the pastel dinner jackets and ruffled and embroidered pink shirts; he was like a shop-worn box that had been left too long on the shelf. The girls wore corsages of sweetheart roses, and the boys wore carnation boutonnieres. The student decorators had managed to create a false ceiling in the gym with streamers and burlap, but the darkness that was necessary for the romantic effect made Byron nervous. Strangers could not easily be seen entering the dark corners near the doors.

The student council members and class officers came to pay their respects to him. Judy Evans strolled over with Mose in tow. "You did it again, Mr. Ashford. This is great! See what a good time everybody's having. Everything's cool! *No problem!*" Judy passed her level palms across the air in her familiar gesture of victory, as if she were stroking the back of an invisible pony; but Byron didn't feel the same elation that he'd experienced at the sports banquet nor the same peace.

"It's good, Judy. It's another step. You and Mose are a great looking couple." Judy wore the same dress that she'd bought for the homecoming game. She couldn't afford another formal gown like the white girls.

After nine o'clock the boys and girls who weren't going steady moved apart into boys' groups and girls' groups, as if the presence of members of the opposite gender couldn't be tolerated for more than a couple of hours.

On the way to the refreshment table Byron saw that one of the white cheerleaders was dancing on a dare with a black basketball player. They kept a safe distance between their bodies, but other couples drew back to watch them and whisper, and even those who also danced turned toward them. They greatly enjoyed the notoriety and smiled smugly at attracting everyone's attention. Byron thought he could read a look of annoyance in Judy's face as she watched them; and he recalled Dad's words, "The trouble with mixin' the races is that the sorriest Negras and the white trash are the ones that'll get together and cause problems for everybody. Soon as we allow blacks and whites to socialize one of them Hammersouths from down at the railroad tracks'll start livin' with a colored woman and then people'll start killin' one another. It's the riffraff that'll mix—white people your mother wouldn't let in the front door." Byron felt guilty for remembering Dad's words as if they were his own secret thoughts and true sentiments; but the incident passed quickly, and Byron began to share Judy's elated appraisal of triumph.

Sometime after eleven o'clock Byron had already begun saying goodnight to the faculty. He experienced the full, happy, satisfied, sleepy feeling that one has after a large meal with several glasses of wine among good friends. The prom had been a success. The students proved that they could enjoy an integrated event without any problems. It was a small step, an important small step, toward doing normal and natural things again, now together. If they could only multiply these small steps, they would once again be able to communicate and participate as one community, as they had before within the white community, with understanding and sympathy and care for one another, but now with equal participation of blacks and whites together.

Then something exploded like a bottle that had been thrown from the top of seats of the gymnasium; but Byron was aware that the crash came at the opposite end of the gymnasium, near the rest rooms and the dressing rooms, in the darkest corner, beside the door to Earl Harris's office under the basketball goal. Earl was near the electric panel, and Byron shouted for him to switch on all the lights and not to allow anyone to leave by the back door. By the time Byron reached the back of the gym the lights had begun to come on, one at a time, destroying the fantasies and romance that the students had labored many hours to produce. Apparently the flying glass came from something like a Molotov cocktail tossed through the small back door that was ordinarily used only by coaches and players. A motor raced and wheels crunched on the gravel outside. A group of student vigilantes ran toward the door. Byron blocked them.

"No one is to leave the building."

"Mr. Ashford, you're letting them get away! You shouldn't stop us from going outside."

"That's the police's business. Don't go out there. Randy, you and Mr. Arnold go call the police and tell them what has happened. Hurry it up. Maybe they can stop the car in town." Byron had noticed that Earl Harris leaving the building alone immediately after he'd turned on the lights. "Is anyone hurt?"

Julie Hemphill shouted that a girl's arm had been slightly glazed by a piece of glass from the bottle, but first aid was being applied, and no one else was injured.

The prom was scheduled to end at twelve thirty, but Byron extended it until one o'clock in order to let the students talk and unwind, and he allowed the students to leave the building at eleven thirty. He turned off some of the lights again but left enough burning to illuminate the dark corners. Judy Evans came by and stared silently at him with an anger and sorrow too old for her young face. They never spoke again that night, but others spoke incessantly, three and four at once in tight circles, so that no one really heard what anyone else was saying.

At twelve forty-five Byron asked for quiet and pleaded for everyone to go straight home. Earl handed him a slip of paper torn off the back of an envelope. "It was that green Studebaker again. I got part of the license plate number. I couldn't read it all."

After he reached his mother's apartment Byron sat in a chair beside the telephone still dressed in his tuxedo hoping that the phone wouldn't ring and waiting for dawn. He wondered how many others in town stayed awake through the night hoping for a peaceful sunrise. The students probably slept, lulled by excitement, as good a soporific as any other for the very young. He hoped that Judy Evans was sleeping. He hoped that he could make her believe that her prom had still been a success, a bitter success perhaps, a victorious battle in a long war that was ongoing. He hoped that he could make himself believe that it had still been a victory, so that he could convince others.

Then Byron almost hoped that the telephone would ring or even the shrill yelping of hounds might shatter the stillness of the night. He remembered the night that Uncle Percy had died, when the ringing of the telephone had cracked the cold, brittle night and shattered it. Now he seemed to hold the sleepless darkness carefully in his consciousness like a fragile crystal that might slip and smash at any moment, but nothing broke the fearful silence, and nothing more happened the night of the prom, except for the seeds of fear and hatred that were planted and began to sprout secretly.

The morning light dissolved his fear or at least made it invisible in the sunlight. The eyes of the soul see some things only in the darkness, and they are blinded in the light. Whether real truth lies in the day or in the night, Byron was grateful for the dawn, when the eyes of the soul sleep and somnambulate through the waking sunny days while fleshly eyes watch pretty things outside in the bright, bobbling world. It was perhaps easier to face the realities of the day than the fear and phantoms of the night, and the first reality to be faced was checking the license plate number of the green Studebaker at DeLane's car lot.

WHEN BYRON ARRIVED AT the car lot a little after nine o'clock on Saturday morning DeLane was standing in the doorway of his tiny shed office with his arms crossed, leaning against the doorjamb. He neither uncrossed his arms to wave nor spoke nor smiled, as he usually did when Byron approached him; but DeLane followed Byron with his eyes as he walked across the lot between the cars. If Byron had to confront him, this was the place to do it, where no pleasant memories and no happy associations lingered. He circled the rusting metal parts and aging, broken, obsolete hulks until he reached their fishing car. The license plate matched the numbers that Earl has scratched on the torn edge from the back of an envelope.

"Whad'cha want, Byron?"

"I need to talk with you about the prom."

"I done got me a date." The words were vintage DeLane, but still there was no smile.

"Did you hear about the bomb?"

"Yeah. I heerd you had a little ruckus. About what I'd perdict with Niggers and whites dancin' together. Nobody got hurt." His arms, like freshly hewn tree trunks stripped of their bark, were still crossed as if he were barring the door to prevent Byron from entering; and Byron was glad DeLane didn't invite him inside to sit down. He wanted to stand and face him here in the yard.

"Did you have anything to do with it or know anything about it?"

DeLane stared at him for a long time. At first Byron thought he saw contempt on DeLane's face, but then it seemed that he hadn't heard the question or perhaps hadn't understood it. Byron considered repeating his words when DeLane finally spoke. "Maybe. Maybe not. Why're you askin'?"

"Someone spotted an old green Studebaker scratching off from the school right after it happened."

"'r ol' fishin' car?" DeLane's voice was mocking, teasing in the old familiar way, but still without a trace of his usual mirth or laughter or even a smile. "They's a bunch of boys knows where I keep the keys to the old heaps and a right smart of 'em don't like Niggers and whites dancin' together no more 'an I do."

"I know that our old fishing car was involved. I haven't told the police chief yet, but I'm going to call him as soon as I get back to town."

"Don't go and do that, Byron."

"Why not? Are you involved in some way?"

"That's fer me to know and fer you to find out. What if I am? Would you go and tell on me?"

"I'd have to."

"Why's that?"

"Because it's the right thing to do. I couldn't do anything else."

"Well, I done hit. I throwed a little fireworks in the gym last night. Hit was me, but if yo're really my friend you won't go and tell on me."

"I have to, DeLane, unless you go and confess yourself. I'll go with you. I'll stand right beside you and help you any way I can."

"I ain't about to do that. You'll have to do hit and go and turn me in like some Nigger lovin' bastard that's chose them over me. Don't go and do hit, Byron. Nobody got hurt. I was drunk and half outa my mind when I heerd about that Nigger dancin' with a white girl. Don't do hit."

"I have to."

"Well, ain't that a fine howdy-do, and all yer talk about bein' my friend since we was just li'le boys."

"I am your friend, DeLane. I'd do anything in the world for you, but there comes a time when something is more important than friendship, something really important."

"And you done chose the Niggers over me, over somebody who's took kere of you and loved you like you was my own brother, more 'an I loved my own brothers."

"I had to know whether you were directly involved before I told the police."

"Don't go and do hit, Byron. Don't go and call the law on me. Leastways let somebody else do hit, if hit's got to be done."

"I can't. I'll help you and stand by you any way I can, but it's my responsibility to report it."

"Well, ain't that a purdy howdy-do." They were Dally's words gathered up from long ago and flung out at Byron like slop that had grown moldy in a zinc bucket kept for the hogs. "Don't you never come around here and talk to me ag'in." DeLane turned and went inside the shed and slammed the door.

Since he was a little boy Byron had imagined this scene hundreds, even thousands of times with their positions reversed. He'd believed that someday DeLane would reject him and betray him. He'd never thought that he could ever reject and betray DeLane. More than anyone else in the world DeLane had always accepted him and understood him and loved

him for who he was. Rejecting and betraying DeLane was the last thing
he ever wanted to do, but DeLane interpreted his accusation as a personal
rejection and betrayal. In some way Byron believed he was being forced to
reject and betray DeLane by forces and events beyond his intention, out of
his control. Byron felt desolate and abandoned and alone in the world, as
if some immunity from evil had been snatched away from him.

ON MONDAY OF THE last week of the academic year Earl Harris came into
Byron's office without knocking, because he was holding two bottles of Coca-
cola, one in each hand with no knuckles free for rapping on the glass with
the gold lettering, "Principal's Office." Earl held them up like champagne
for toasting and then handed one to Byron. The broad grin almost seemed
to break apart his usually expressionless wooden face.

"He's in jail, the bastard. I should've listened to you a long time ago.
Thanks, my friend."

It was the first time that Earl had called Byron his friend; and on some
other day, on some other occasion, it would have made Byron happy. Today it
only increased his anguish by reminding him that his truest friend was in jail.

"Thanks." Byron took the coke and immediately began sipping it, so
that he wouldn't have to say anything.

"You look mighty glum."

"I'm glad you and your family are safe. I'm glad it's over, but it came at
a price for me."

"You lost your fishing buddy. That's too bad. I guess you'll miss going
to the river with him."

"Yes, it was an important part of my life."

"Maybe you didn't really know him."

"Maybe not," Byron replied politely, but he thought, *but I knew him
much more deeply than I'll ever know you, and he knows more than you'll ever
know about who I am.*

"You did good, real good." When Byron looked down at his desk and
failed to respond after several minutes, Earl stood up and held up his coke.
"Cheers! I better get along. I see you're busy."

Byron didn't even look up or say goodbye. It was not until he heard the door close and click that he realized that tears were running down his cheeks.

BYRON WANTED TO SPARE his mother the news of DeLane's incarceration, but he was unaware of her sometimes mysterious sources of information, even now in her weakened state of health from the chemo treatments. Her channels to local events were enhanced by the return of Elmo and Tancy to Morganville. Elmo completed the cycle of communication between himself and Irene Ashford and J. W. Moss. Irene also sought to spare her son from the pain of acknowledging and discussing DeLane as the culprit, because she knew that Byron had played a role in the accusations that put DeLane in jail; and so she never mentioned it.

At least once a week Elmo stopped by Irene Ashford's apartment with fresh vegetables from his garden.

"They say you don't have no appetite, Miss Reen, but I know you can eat a mess o' Tancy's peas. She cooked 'em good with a ham bone, just like her Maw used to do, like you likes 'em."

"They smell wonderful. Thank you, Elmo; you're so good to us. I think I might even be able to take a few bites. I haven't been able to eat at all lately. It's not just the treatments. I'm grieving over DeLane Moss. Do you know anything about that?"

"J. W. he's talked to me a little. He's all broke up."

"So is Byron, but I daren't say a word. I think DeLane was the best friend he ever had."

"Yes'um, I knows about that, too. I believes they was real good fo' one another. They sorta brought out the best in one another, as the man says."

"Byron! When did you come in? How long have you been standing out there in the hall?"

"Long enough. I was trying to keep you from finding out."

"I know, dear. I felt like it was hard for you to talk about."

Byron gave his mother a hug and was aware that tears once again dropped down his cheeks. "It's hard, Mother; it's really hard."

"I know, dear." Irene Ashford held him against her breast for a while as if he were still a baby, which she felt he was. Then she pushed him away gently and turned to Elmo. "I can't understand it, Elmo. DeLane was such a bright boy. I always thought he was the smartest one of the Mosses, surely the best looking. What do you think happened to him?"

"Not nothin' happen, Miss Reen. That's how I sees it. J. W. he changed and made up to all o' us. Byron he growed up to be a right fine man. Me and Tancy got on with our lives, but DeLane he jus' stay the same. He don't never change, and that's the whole problem, as I sees it. Not nothing happen wif DeLane. He jus' never move on."

As Elmo left, Byron walked out to the front stoop with him.

"Thank you for coming, Elmo. Mother appreciates your visits more than I can ever tell you. I do, too. It's so good to have you back close to us."

"It mean a whole lot to us, too, me an' Tancy. You don't never get close to other folks like them as what you knowed as a boy. Ain't that right?"

"That's exactly right. You've helped me sort out what's gone on with DeLane more than anybody else, and I thank you for that most of all. Do you have any advice about what I can do to help?"

"Go see J. W. He need you right now."

"What about DeLane? Can I do anything for him?"

"I'd ax J. W. 'bout that, if I was you. Go see him, Mista Byron. He really need you right now."

"What can I do to make you stop calling me Mister?"

"Old habits they die hard. Don't know as I can ever quit on that one."

THE SECOND WEEK OF June, after the academic year ended, Morganville High School was inhabited only by janitors, painters, carpenters, and the principal. Its doors and windows were flung open, and dust and scraped-off paint and debris erupted in clouds at irregular intervals; but the principal's office was closed and sealed, like a tomb in the midst of an ant hill; and the air conditioner ran noisily in the window. Byron had phoned J. W. Moss's office at the lumberyard and wasn't surprised when J. W. returned his call and asked to stop by to see him at the high school.

"Kere if I smoke?" J. W. took out one of his vile cigars.

"It's your school now, more than mine. After all you're on the board. Oh, I didn't mean that the way it came out, J. W. Sure. Smoke. It's all right with me."

"I reckin you was wantin' to talk about DeLane." J. W. began turning his hat round and round, measuring out the edge of the brim by inches from his left thumb and forefinger to his right thumb and forefinger. The gesture had replaced pawing the ground as his favored nervous habit when he was talking about things he dreaded and feared. Byron wished he'd also developed some such habit, so that he would have something to occupy his hands and eyes.

"It's awful. You can't imagine how terrible I feel."

"Reckin I can. I know how much stock you put in DeLane."

"Maybe I shouldn't have told the police. Maybe I could have let some-one else do it."

"You couldn't do no different. It was yer job."

"How can I help him? Is there anything he needs that I can . . . ? Could I go visit him?"

J. W. tucked his head and shook it slowly from side to side. "He won't talk to you. He won't let 'em put you on the visitors' list. I done ast him. I thought maybe if y'all talked . . ."

"I wanted to see him, but I wouldn't know what to say."

"I know. He's bad hurt. I never seen him so low, but you couldn't he'p it. You done what you had to do."

"Will I have to testify against him in court? My God, that would be so awful . . ."

"Not gonna be no trial. He's gonna plead guilty, partways I reckin 'cause he don't want to have you tellin' all what he did to his face before the judge."

Once again Byron began to tear. "I'm sorry, J. W."

"That's awright, son."

"Will he go to prison? Will he have to spend a long time . . . ?"

"I don't believe so. I done talked to the D. A. and the judge. I figure he'll get a few months. I got him a good lawyer, one from out of town, from Atlanter. I pro'bly could've already bailed him out, but I thought he needed to stay in jail right now and think about what he done."

"People could have gotten hurt. Some people did suffer, Earl Harris and his family."

"That's just hit. DeLane, he don't realize . . ."

"Why did he do it, J. W.? What possessed him?"

"He just never growed up. You growed up, and I growed up, but DeLane he never quite growed up."

"In some ways I think I've never grown up either. I still wanted him to like me, to get his approval."

"Well, I reckin none of us grows up in some way or t'other, but if'n we don't grow up the right ways, hit's more serious, if people gets hurt and put in danger. I done some bad thangs, but I tried to make up fer 'em, best ways I could. They's some thangs I done to you and DeLane I'm sorry fer now. I hope you'll fergive me."

"I misjudged you, too, J. W., for too long; but I still owe DeLane a lot. Do you think he'll forgive me? Do you think he'll ever speak to me again?"

"I don't rightly know, Byron. I doubt it, knowin' how he is. Maybe a few weeks in jail will do him some good, but I sorta doubt it."

"Will you tell him I'm thinking about him, that if there's anything I can do for him, . . . that I love him like a brother." Now Byron was weeping openly.

"Yeah. I will, Byron. I'll be shore to. Oh, they's one more thing. I need to git his boat from up at the river. I'm havin' to take kere of his cars and thangs. I got somebody to run the lot till we decide what to do about hit."

Byron opened the kneehole drawer of his desk and pulled out his key to the boathouse. "Here's the key . . ."

"Oh, I don't need that. I done got DeLane's key. I was just wantin' to git yer permission."

"Hell, you don't need no permission for Canebrake Beach." Byron repeated DeLane's words and grammar and began sobbing.

J. W. rose, but he didn't embrace Byron as DeLane might have done. "I know, Byron. Hit's mighty hard fer you, fer all of us. You was like a brother to me, too, a little brother, but yer feelin's warn't the same."

THREE DAYS LATER BYRON went to the river by himself. He unlocked the boathouse, hoping the boat might still be inside, even though he knew it would be empty. Byron felt empty, too, like the boathouse, with the river lapping softly between the boards at his feet, where the boat had been, where it would never be again, where DeLane would never be again in his life. He locked the door, even though there was nothing inside to protect and secure. Then he walked out to the river's edge and sat down on the sand and listened to the river cane rustling and clacking in the breeze. His eyes were dry. Byron hadn't wept since J. W. left his office on Monday morning, and he never wept again for DeLane.

Byron undressed and stealthily slipped out of his underpants and tee shirt, as if people were watching him and staring at the lump on his spine, as if he could hear DeLane saying, "I don't kere about yer old hump; hit don't make no nevermind to me," and laugh to make him feel better, healed and whole. The river current sounded like laughter, like DeLane's laughter.

Then Byron waded into the river, up to his ankles, up to his knees, up to his groin, up to his waist, up to his breasts, up to his shoulders. He thought about ducking under the water and never coming back up, about being absorbed into the stream; and he did dive down under the surface, under the rippling current. For a few seconds he felt as one with the river, as one with the world, as one with the universe. Then he broke back into the air and gasped and saw the blurred vision of green leaves above his head and their shadows and the sun's reflected light far out on the water.

Byron swam and trudged back to the bank and pulled himself along until he reached the sand and sat naked and dripping with his head tucked between his knees. He asked himself why the one man who had known him and understood him and respected him and admired him and accepted him and loved him completely as he was could not have given at least a small acknowledgment of those gifts to people whose skin was a different color. Byron's deformed back never repulsed DeLane, never seemed to bother him even enough to notice it, but darker skins enraged him. *Why?*

Byron was never able to find an answer to his question.

## EPILOGUE 1971–2000

In the fall of 1971 Byron Ashford agreed to continue as Principal of Morganville High School for the following year and settled permanently in Morganville after he and Sally Rutledge were married in the spring. When the city and county schools merged, he became Principal of Davis County High School. J. W. Moss stayed on the city school board and was elected chairman of the county board after the merger. Byron and J. W. worked together to create one of the most progressive school systems in the state. In 2000, the year that Byron retired, he was recognized with the Georgia Educator of the Year Award. Although he never finished his doctoral dissertation from Vanderbilt on the poetry of the Carolinian divines, he did receive a doctorate in school administration by attending many summer sessions at Georgia State University in Atlanta.

J. W. Moss became one of the wealthiest men in north Georgia. He used his lumberyard to launch a building supply company that eventually opened branches all over the state of Georgia and even in eastern Alabama.

In 1972 Earl Harris accepted a coaching position in Atlanta. His basketball teams won so many state championships that Byron lost count of them. Byron and Earl saw each other occasionally at professional conferences. Although they continued to exchange Christmas cards, their friendship became just a polite acquaintance within a few years.

Irene Ashford lived to see Byron and Sally married. Although she died while Sally was pregnant with their first child, Irene knew that it was a girl and would be named for her. Her delight in her son's marriage and the anticipation of the birth of her granddaughter undergirded the happiest year of her life.

Mose and Judy continued to date after they went to the University of Georgia, he on an athletic scholarship and she on an academic scholarship. They broke up during their sophomore year. After she graduated, Judy moved to California, where she married and reared her family; she rarely visited Morganville. Mose became a professional football player of considerable renown; and his generous support of the Davis County schools, both financial and personal, was one of the factors in their success. Mose was a frequent and greatly adored speaker at Davis County sports banquets.

Elmo and Tancy Jones continued to enjoy their retirement in Morgan-ville. They were attentive and almost daily visitors during Irene Ashford's last weeks of life. Elmo and J. W. often traveled together to sporting events, especially to see Mose play. Although the Joneses and Mosses ate supper together several times a year, Sylvia and Tancy remained rather cautious and suspicious of one another.

DeLane Moss was released from prison for good behavior after serving a little more than four months—he'd been sentenced to a six months term. He moved his used cars to south Georgia and opened a lot near Albany. Like his elder brother he expanded his business and over the years pur-chased several other lots and became moderately wealthy, although he was far less successful than J. W. DeLane never became a father, but he adored his nephew, J. W. and Sylvia's son Donny, who was his frequent fishing partner. Although Byron heard that DeLane had visited J. W. and Sylvia in Morganville several times, Byron and DeLane never saw each other again after DeLane's arrest.

In 1975 Byron sold the last part of the Ashford farm, the property that had been used as a pasture where the giant oaks grew, where he'd ridden his horse, and the land on the river that his family had always called Canebrake Beach. When Byron and Sally's son was born three years after the birth of their daughter Irene, people could never understand why they named him DeLane.

# Maud's Heirs

It was not that I loved my grandson more than my three granddaughters, but he was the only boy and was named for me and so he had a special place in my life and my heart. We weren't sure he'd live more than a few days when he was born with a severe heart defect; and my daughter told me with a shaky voice and terrified eyes, "Daddy, maybe we shouldn't name him for you, like we planned . . . in case he doesn't make it," and then burst into full sobs and pulsing quakes in my arms. I insisted that he bear my name for however long he breathed on this earth, and I cradled him and rocked him for hours and days following his surgeries, especially after my son-in-law was diagnosed with cancer in what seemed to us a cosmically cruel blow of fate in a brief span of time.

*Could this strapping six foot two athlete have once been that fragile baby?*

When David called to tell me that he was engaged, I heard the familiar mixture of excitement and anxiety in his voice. We had long been able to hear each other's moods and states of being over the telephone, from his years of prep school through college to law school, and now in his seventy hour a week labors trying to secure a permanent position with a prominent group of Atlanta lawyers.

And now I was fussing and fretting like a high school beauty contestant before a pageant. What to wear? What to serve? What dishes to use? Why on God's earth had I insisted on their coming for lunch? I'd managed for myself very ably in my small apartment in the retirement center since Eleanor's death; but I rarely—almost never—attempted to entertain with anything more than a cup of coffee and a plate of cookies. Eleanor would have taken care of everything, even laid out clothes for me, and allowed me to sit with David and Celia and enjoy their company while she prepared and served delicious food with perfect timing and elegant presentation.

*Keep it simple, Dave,* I said to myself over and over the morning before my grandson's visit. *You have some good chicken salad and rolls and cookies from the deli. All you need to do is cut up celery and slice a lemon and make Eleanor's tomato aspic—you've got the recipe—and brew some iced tea, which you've done a thousand times.*

The morning sped by as I tried to follow my own internal directions. *Dear heavens above, is the doorbell chiming already? I haven't even changed my shirt.* It took me so long to find the towel to dry my hands that I was still holding it when I opened the door.

David smothered me in a bear hug, as he always did.

"Gramps, I love you"—his usual greeting; and he started through the doorway leaving his fiancée in the hall, as if he'd forgotten she was there.

"Aren't you going to introduce me?"

"Oh! Gramps, this is Celia."

She was the most beautiful woman I'd ever seen—the second most beautiful, I corrected myself. She kissed me on my cheek as she took my hand, as if she'd always known me, and I felt her long lashes brush against my ear.

"David's talked about you from the moment we met. I think you're the most important person in the world to him."

"Not any more, my dear, now that he has you." They clasped each other's hands and peered into each other's eyes with the gaze only young lovers can share, but David glanced back toward me with an equal effusion of love. "I'm so very happy for you." And I added, so that I wouldn't melt into sentimental tears, "You know he can be a scoundrel sometimes."

They appeared to be opposites, not because Dave's skin was white and Celia's was brown, but because her almost black eyes like sparkling onyx contrasted so greatly with his pale blue eyes, like Aunt Maud's eyes, that even Celia's angular, almost delicate beauty and his muscular, heavy frame seemed less different than their eyes. He'd put on too many pounds the last couple of years since he'd been working at the law firm and was almost but not quite yet overweight. Celia reminded me of David as a baby, as the little boy that was forever being cajoled to eat.

"Can I get you something to drink and snack on? A Coke or sherry? Lunch will be very simple."

"I'll take a Coke." David made his usual request.

"A glass of sherry would be nice. We had a big breakfast. We don't need anything more to eat." Celia shot a quick glance at David; she was obviously monitoring his added pounds. "Thank you, Mister . . . what should I call you?"

"Could you manage *Gramps* like my other grandchildren?"

"*Gramps*. Of course. How kind to include me in their company."

As Celia sipped her sherry I felt as if I'd seen her, known her somewhere before; and I almost asked if we'd met or tried to explore some chance gathering where we'd been together, when she answered the itch of my questing recognition.

"I don't know if David told you that our families have a connection from the past. My grandmother's college scholarship was sponsored by your aunt." Celia smiled.

I was so stunned that I could hardly speak. "So! You're Ruby's granddaughter. No, David never mentioned . . . No wonder you look so familiar."

DAVE SAW RUBY ONLY a few times as a teenager when he was visiting Aunt Maud in Nashville. Of course he remembered her from her dramatic rescue as a baby when Aunt Maud had probably saved her life after she was struck by the train, and they'd played together as small children. After he entered Vanderbilt he was often at Aunt Maud's home on weekends, and it wasn't unusual to encounter Ruby coming or going, but he never expected to see her during the sit-in demonstration at the federal courthouse. It was as if he were seeing her for the first time—vital and beautiful and alluring, not as the injured child grown up.

He knew that Aunt Maud was paying for Ruby's college expenses at Fisk and wondered whether she would cut off Ruby's scholarship if she learned about her involvement in "The Movement." Aunt Maud contributed to the cost of Dave's university tuition, too; but he wouldn't have had to drop out of school if she cut him off, as Ruby would have to do.

Dave remembered his mother asking Aunt Maud why she was sending "that Negra girl" to school, and Aunt Maud told her that "Papa always said we have an obligation to take care of the darkies as long as we live together and they take care of us. Ruby's a right intelligent Negra for the kinds of things her race can learn, and they need some good teachers for the colored schools."

Dave's mother had told him about a sit-in demonstration at a restaurant in their hometown several months before he and Ruby had joined the group at the federal courthouse. Aunt Maud was greatly disturbed that such a thing could take place in the town where she and Dave's mother had grown up. In fact, she called it "disgusting." "Self-respecting colored people have too much pride to behave like that," she'd told his mother over the phone. "Mark my words, the Negras that get ahead in the world and make something of themselves are those that know their place."

Dave had been tempted to tell Aunt Maud about his participation in a sit-in. It would almost have been worth losing her financial support to shock her and let her know who he really was and what he believed in.

When Dave joined the sit-in at the federal courthouse in Nashville where he and Ruby reconnected, they began talking as they'd never talked before. He was amazed at her insights about T. S. Eliot, his current literary hero. She even seemed to understand the allusions in *Four Quartets* better than he did.

Now Dave knew he could never let Aunt Maud know about his participation in the sit-in demonstrations, lest she find out about Ruby's involvement, too. He could survive without Aunt Maud's financial help, but Ruby would more likely have to drop out of college. He admitted to himself that he was also afraid of incurring Aunt Maud's wrath upon himself, not just the financial aspects of her support.

In front of the federal courthouse the demonstrators dwindled by the late afternoon. At closing time a few were arrested, and the others who remained were driven out and gathered in a nearby park. At dusk some tents and sleeping bags were brought to the park for the diminishing remnant. Ruby and Dave talked on and on—he hadn't intended to stay past dark— like two isolated pilgrims who had met in a desert. By midnight Dave and Ruby were left alone in a tent and huddled together in the chilly night air.

Dave couldn't remember when they began to kiss and explore each other's bodies; their lovemaking seemed to evolve seamlessly out of their daylong conversation. Neither of them planned or even understood how they began intercourse, still clothed against the cold. It was the first time for both of them. It was something both of them had pledged to defer until a full and reasoned and agreed upon commitment was made within an exclusive relationship.

In the days that followed Dave was obsessed with the fear that he had impregnated Ruby. He called her several times a day, and they met every day. He assured her that he would marry her if she was pregnant, and she reassured him over and over that she was not pregnant. He told her that he wanted to marry her anyway, and she smiled at him and said nothing. Within a few weeks they saw each other less and less frequently, and as weeks became months their visits were rare. They continued to talk rapturously when they did meet, about T. S. Eliot and other poets living and dead; but they never kissed again nor touched each other intimately.

For the rest of his life Dave often dreamed about Ruby. He told Eleanor about their tryst with full disclosure and complete details before they married, and the revelation seemed to draw them closer emotionally, but Dave never told Eleanor all of his true feelings for Ruby. Even now as an old man, Dave remembered Ruby as his first love, a love like no other in his life.

*Is it possible that Celia is really Ruby's granddaughter? Is such a coincidence even possible after all these years?*

"Gramps, can I give you a hand in the kitchen?"

"You stay here with your sweetheart. I can get things together. We shouldn't leave Celia all alone."

"She can read some of your short stories. Gramps will forgive anything in the world except not reading his books."

"I've read a couple of your books that David loaned me. I loved them. They reminded me of my grandmother's writing." There were more reasons than Celia could ever guess that Ruby's stories sounded like mine. Celia picked up my most recent publication from where I'd left it in prominent view on the lamp table beside the sofa for any visitor to see immediately. "But I haven't read this one."

I suddenly realized that David might have something he wanted to say to me in private. "All right then. As long as you don't groan loudly enough for us to hear you in the next room."

"Gramps, don't you have any better plates than these faded ones? They've been through the dishwasher one time too many."

"Those are the ones I picked out after I learned who Celia's grand-mother was. They were Aunt Maud's." (They were the plates Ruby and I used when we had supper together at Aunt Maud's house when my aunt was vacationing in Florida. Ruby began to set out the plates on the kitchen table for the sandwiches we'd brought from the deli. I said, "Let's eat in the dining room." And Ruby smiled in that coy way that crinkled her eyes as if she were about to wink and pressed the corners of her lips together. "Miss Maud wouldn't let me eat in the dining room." "That's all the more reason for us to eat there tonight." I'd almost added "as equals," but Ruby would've broken one of those plates over my head.) Now the little violets were faded and the green leaves were almost invisible and the gold borders remained only on parts of the rims.

"You're an old sentimentalist, Gramps."

"What is it you wanted to tell me?"

David moved around the counter and gave me another bear hug. "You can still read my mind, can't you, just like you did when I was a little boy? Am I just marrying Celia out of rebellion, to show, you know . . . people?"

"And what *does* your mother have to say about it?"

"That's it, isn't it? She's *the people* I meant."

"I'm afraid my liberalism didn't rub off on my daughter. It skipped a generation. How's she responding?"

"She's polite. Very, very polite. She talks about Celia to her friends as if she was Mother Teresa, Oprah, Halle Berry and Princess Diana all rolled into one."

"That's not a good sign."

"I know."

"Does it matter to you?"

"Of course."

"How much?"

"I don't know. That's what I want you to tell me."

"You love your mother, and you love Celia. If one relationship has to be strained and compromised, which one will it be?"

"Mother's."

I thought I could see the beginning of tears in David's eyes. "Can you live with that?"

"Yes."

"Well, Vabo,"—my baby name for him—"you've given the right answers. The rest of it is up to you. You've got to work it out inside yourself and with Celia, and let the chips fall where they may."

"But it isn't easy, Gamp"—his baby name for me.

"I know. I know more than you could ever imagine."

DAVE HAD HEARD PEOPLE say that Maud Jeffers had been a strikingly beautiful young woman, not as a Hollywood glamour puss, but with a serene beauty that people perceived more and more fully as they came to know her. They had spoken about how her skin glowed like pearls. Maud Jeffers had married the only son of one of Tennessee's wealthiest families that owned a string of hardware stores in four states. Maud had met him in college, and they had married the day after they graduated, and he had died of cancer less than two years after their wedding, not unlike Dave's son-in-law two generations later. Maud had no children.

Maud had laid aside her fashionable clothes and donned the wool suits and cotton shirtwaist dresses hemmed at mid-calf, appearing even longer with her flat-heeled shoes. She'd cut her long auburn hair and curled it into tight ringlets against her scalp that looked like the natural hair of many black people who tried to reverse the process and straighten their hair into long flowing tresses. Within a decade Maud's hair had turned grey, as if it was imitating her clothes and general demeanor.

Maud had feigned ignorance and helplessness as the sudden head of a large company and ceaselessly asked that people tell her what to do; but she'd gone into the office every day. People on the inside knew that the company not only thrived and grew under her direction but also might have foundered without her wise decisions.

Every summer Maud came to visit the family in Dave's hometown in Georgia for two weeks, and her mother, Dave's grandmother, accompanied her back to Nashville to spend a month. Aunt Maud kept up with all the black families her father had assisted during his lifetime. When Dave was seven years old his mother and Aunt Maud took him shopping downtown. As they traversed the two blocks of stores on the main street, a large black woman came up to them and caught Aunt Maud's arm.

"Lawdy, Miss Maud. Lawdy mussy me. You done come back home." Aunt Maud asked about all her children and her relatives and her back trouble and told the woman that she couldn't get down to her house on this trip but promised to see her on the next trip. They went on talking and talking while people walked around them on the sidewalk; and Dave's mother looked embarrassed and stood back apart from them against the building holding his hand. The black woman turned to his mother and said, "Miss Maud she be the angel of mussy. She give me the moneys to cure my baby when he nigh to dyin'."

His mother look chagrined and muttered something like, "That's nice. I'm so glad." Aunt Maud and the black woman went on talking in loud voices. Finally his mother said, "Maud, we've got to get to the store."

"Go on, then. I'll meet you back at the car. I haven't seen Maybelle in, let's see, two or was it three years ago on my summer visit? And we need to catch up."

After Dave's grandmother died, and he was in the fourth grade, he seemed to take her place for the month-long visit with Aunt Maud in Nashville following her two week visit with his family in Georgia.

Aunt Maud had hired Walter, Ruby's uncle, to work a few hours a week in her garden. Within six months Walter was working halftime and assisting the aged cook with cleaning chores inside the house. Within a year he was working full time and having both his Noon dinner and his late afternoon supper in Aunt Maud's kitchen.

Dave enjoyed his summer visit to Nashville. He learned to swim at the country club pool—there was no swimming pool in his hometown. He played with other boys and girls his age around the pool; but no children lived in Aunt Maud's neighborhood. Dave's only companion there was

Walter, who taught him to whittle as well as buck dance and hambone to Aunt Maud's delight and his mother's horror. Walter had the strongest body and the most perfect male physique that Dave had ever seen. He was much stronger and more handsome than the pictures of Charles Atlas that boys his age admired and envied from the back pages of comic books.

Years later when Dave gazed at the statue of Michelangelo's David in Florence, his namesake that he'd longed all his life to see in its original after looking at photographs of it in art magazines, he immediately thought of Walter, whose torso it could well have been if the statue had been painted black. Walter's skin was darker than Ruby's, like chiseled obsidian, almost as dark as Ruby's eyes; but his features were thin and fine and his fingers were long and agile as he manipulated a knife to carve wooden animals or twisted string to form a cat's cradle.

One afternoon as Dave started to walk through the dining room toward the kitchen to get a Coke out of the refrigerator, he saw Aunt Maud half hiding behind the drapes looking out into the garden where Walter seemed to be rising naked out of the flowers that came almost to his navel. Dave waited silently and observed her. She was so transfixed that she didn't even notice him behind her. She didn't usually fidget at all, but then she picked at her fingers until her cuticles began to bleed, but she still didn't see him. Dave called to her, and she turned, startled, almost gasping as the ringlets beside her ears bobbed back and forth, and he remembered the afternoon his mother had suddenly opened the door of his bedroom and found him looking at pictures of female underwear models in the Sears and Roebuck catalogue.

"Oh, Dave! I just wanted to be sure that Walter was getting his work done. Not loafing around."

"Walter always works hard. You don't have to check up on him."

"Yes, that's so."

Dave forgot about the Coke and went back to his bedroom and gazed down at Walter as Aunt Maud had. Walter never looked up, and the spell was unbroken for almost half an hour. If he could be strong like Walter, Dave had thought, he wouldn't mind being a Negro.

It wasn't unusual for Aunt Maud to sit with Walter at the kitchen table after he'd finished his supper and talk with him for an hour or even several hours. "He's the only one I can talk to like that," she told Dave. "He's the only one that really understands what's going on."

"Why don't you let him have supper with us in the dining room, so we can visit while we eat, or at least all eat together in the kitchen?"

"Oh, Davey, don't be ridiculous. People don't do things like that." Aunt Maud laughed in her rapid twittering way like a cardinal. "You're just teasing me. You know better. You know it's impossible. It's absurd." Aunt Maud rarely laughed at all in any way, but then she laughed again.

"VABO, ARE YOU GOING to help me clear up?"

"Vabo?" Celia arched her brows

"That's Gramps's baby name for me."

"I'm learning all sorts of new things about you. Can I help?"

"You haven't finished reading Gramps's new story. It has a kicker ending."

"I do want to finish it, and it's nice to have two men waiting on me." Celia pursed her lips just as Ruby would have done after a teasing joke.

With David's help we needed only two trips to bring the dishes into the kitchen. I put the leftover chicken salad into a plastic bowl and found a spot in the refrigerator. "Do you want to scrape or rinse? We could just leave the dishes in the sink. I'll wash them later."

"Let's wash 'em now, if you don't mind. It'll give Celia a chance to finish reading . . . and us a chance to talk a little more."

"Sure thing. Well, wash or dry then?"

"I'll wash. You know where they go in the cabinet."

"You want an apron?" We both laughed. It seemed as absurd to put an apron around this big hulking man as it had seemed to Aunt Maud long ago to sit down with Walter in the dining room.

"Whatever Mom may think, am I trying to prove something to myself, Gramps? Not just to other people. To myself, too?"

"It's still the same question, Vabo. Do you love her? Do you really love her . . . enough?"

"With all my heart. But it's not going to be easy."

"It never is, Vabo. I don't want to tell you what to do. Only you can decide, but I have to tell you that if your love is as deep as I think it is, you'd spend the rest of your life regretting it if you lost it."

"You loved Gamma like that, didn't you."

I hesitated. How much could I tell David without harm, without distortion or prevarication. "I loved Eleanor very deeply. We had a long and beautiful life together. Many joyful years. But there was someone else. Before. Maybe someday I can tell you about her. Not now. I can't. Maybe someday. Maybe not."

"Why Gramps! I never knew that. Was she someone you knew in college? In high school?"

"I can't talk about it now. I'm sorry. Maybe someday. I don't know."

WHEN DAVE WAS SIX years old, the summer before he entered first grade, the two weeks that Aunt Maud allowed herself for a visit approached an end. Aunt Maud began to make plans for returning to Nashville with her mother and began to prevail on Dave's mother and father to return with her for a visit. His father usually drove the family up to Nashville once during the year. Trips to Tennessee to visit Aunt Maud were the only travels of Dave's childhood, except for shopping excursions and his doctor's appointments in Atlanta. It was still wartime, and there was hardly enough gas available for the drive, and Dave's father had responsibilities on the farm. They usually went to Nashville for Thanksgiving or after Christmas, when the fields were fallow.

Then Aunt Maud asked his mother if Dave might go with her, since his father couldn't drive them up in the car. "It would be such a good lesson for him to travel, and he could help me with Mama on the train. It's harder and harder for me to manage her by myself." The combination of her son's being needed and providing an educational opportunity for him was irresistible to his mother, and so the trip was settled. It would be Dave's first trip on a train.

They met the train at the Junction, over twenty miles from their farm. They sat on two benches set back to back inside the depot. The benches were shaped like the pews at the First Presbyterian Church but made of little oak boards with gaps between them instead of smooth solid dark mahogany.

They'd left the farm before the sun came up, because Dave's mother insisted that they get to the depot an hour before the train was scheduled to arrive in case it came early, although it was almost always late.

Trains stopped at the Junction only when a passenger was boarding or getting off. The depot was mostly deserted. Occasionally someone would come in to pick up a package of freight or send one out.

Finally the depot agent ran through the door from his office into the waiting room and shouted, "Train's a'comin'."

Dave's mother began picking up her things slowly and tucking at her hair and straightening out her skirt, and Dave thought that she would never get ready to go outside. "Hurry up! We'll miss seeing the train pull in."

"There's plenty of time, Davey."

"I'm going outside to see."

"No you don't, young man. You wait for us. There's still plenty of time." Dave's father spoke sternly and held Dave by his shoulders.

After interminable seconds and even minutes, they walked out onto the concrete apron between the station and the tracks. Even after the long wait inside, they couldn't see or hear the train once they were outside; and after waiting and looking down the tracks through an early morning fog so thick the buildings in the town were barely visible, Dave asked the depot agent, "Are you sure the train's coming?"

"You'll see hit in a minute."

"Then a tiny speck of light appeared, so faint and dim it might have been a distant lantern or the tiniest star of heaven. They heard the roar and clacking far away, like wind slamming against the windowpanes of Dave's bedroom during a winter storm. His heart began to pound until the great monster loomed before them roaring and screeching and belching smoke and stream. "It's not going to stop. It'll never be able to stop. It can't stop." No one heard him over the thunderous roar and through their own excitement; and even though they held one another's hands, they felt separated and alone. No dragon of ancient times could have been more fearsome or beautiful or terrifying, and Dave felt a tiny trickle against his leg in the chilly morning air.

The train was still moving slowly when a black man in a white coat jumped down, and as it came to a stop he set a small stool under the steps to the passenger car for them to board. Even with the porter on one side of her and Aunt Maud on her other side, Dave's grandmother tottered on the stool and the first step.

At first Dave was disappointed by the inside of the passenger car. It seemed small, hardly larger than the Trailways bus they rode to Atlanta for his doctor's appointments, nothing like what he'd imagined from looking at the huge railroad cars from the outside at the Junction with people sitting in square windows high above his head. The seats had cane backs and bottoms, and Aunt Maud had brought three sofa pillows for Dave and his grandmother and herself.

The first thing Aunt Maud did, before the train started moving, was to call the conductor to turn a seat around so that they could sit facing one another. Dave sat with his back toward the engine, because it made Aunt Maud dizzy to ride backward. Aunt Maud and his grandmother faced him. His mother had packed both a lunch and a supper for them because the trip took nearly twelve hours in those days, and Aunt Maud never ate in the dining car because it was "outrageously expensive for what you got." Aunt Maud had tied his grandmother's head up in a stocking because someone would probably open a window, and the black soot would fly into her wispy white hair and ruin it.

Aunt Maud crocheted edging for pillow slips; but she insisted that Dave refrain from reading because it would ruin his eyes riding backward, even quicker than reading in an automobile, which was bad enough, she said. Dave couldn't see anything that was in front of him and looked backward at the scenes that had already passed by them, so that the trip was like reading a story, in which everything had happened the moment before and there was no way to catch up with the present.

The conductor walked through the car each time before the train stopped, calling out the name of the station. He leaned on the seatbacks first on one side of the aisle and then on the other and staggered like a drunk man. Dave asked if he could go for some water, and he walked down the aisle imitating the gait of the conductor. Aunt Maud said that he must use the restroom while the train was moving, because it dripped down on the tracks and people could see it in a station. He tried to urinate, but he failed. Perhaps the motion inhibited him or the fear that they would pull into a station, as they did every fifteen or twenty minutes, and his yellow urine would still be dripping down, and people would laugh.

When the conductor announced Swan Pond, he begged Aunt Maud to go out to the platform between the cars, so that they could see the swans. Aunt Maud laughed and told Dave that there was nothing to see, but finally she went out with him. She said they could leave his grandmother by herself for a few minutes. There was not a real pond, much less any swans. Aunt Maud laughed at him again and said it was just a name. (As Dave recalled that trip as an adult he remembered the hurtful names Aunt Maud used in addressing black people; and when he had reprimanded her, she'd said, *They're only names, just names that don't mean anything.*) There never had been any swans at that little mud hole, she told him, nothing but hogs that she'd ever seen. Then the train jerked and lurched, and he was afraid of falling off the platform. He clutched at Aunt Maud's hand, and she laughed at him for being such a scaredy cat, but she took his arm when the train lurched again. As the train jerked and began moving, he wet his pants; and he held a coloring book over the spot until it dried, so that Aunt Maud wouldn't know what he'd done.

The train hadn't completely picked up speed when Aunt Maud looked out the window and frowned before she picked up her crocheting again. Then there was a loud screech that sent a chill through Dave, and the train stopped so suddenly that Aunt Maud and his grandmother tumbled across into the seat on top of him.

"We've hit a child." Aunt Maud whispered and gasped. "I saw it walking toward the tracks but thought it had turned back. You wait here. I'll go see." She left through the front of the car and stayed gone. When the train began to move again, his grandmother kept asking him over and over, "Where's Maud gone?"

Finally the conductor came and told them, "The lady who was with you is taking care of the little colored child and said you wasn't to worry none."

The train did not stop again. It ran full speed to Nashville and left people standing at the depots of the stations all along the way holding onto their suitcases and wondering what had happened.

They didn't see Aunt Maud again even when the train pulled into the station in Nashville. Dave and his grandmother waited and waited and looked out the carriage windows into the darkness trying to see Aunt Maud. The railroad car was completely empty, and the lights were dimmed. His grandmother kept asking him, "Where'd Maud go?" and "Ain't we supposed to git off?"

Then Aunt Maud came through the door at the end of the carriage and down the aisle. Her dress was covered in blood from her shoulders down to her knees, and her arms were caked in dried blood. "Maud!" Dave's grandmother said her name so slowly that it seemed to linger in the air, like a fly buzzing around.

"The child's still alive. I don't know whether she'll survive or not. Bad injuries to her legs, and her back all cut up. I had them call ahead to the hospital to have an ambulance meet us. I wouldn't let them stop till we got here, as you know."

"How old is she?" Dave asked. "What happened?"

"The child is probably between three and four years old, I reckon. She just walked onto the tracks. The engineer tried to stop. He pulled her along with the cow catcher." Aunt Maud told them that she'd held the child all the way. She'd waited for the other passengers to leave the train and told the conductor to find the porter to fetch their suitcases so that no more people than necessary would see her bloody clothes.

After a restless night's sleep at Aunt Maud's house, the next day she called the hospital every two hours to inquire about the child, and on the eighth day the hospital reported the she was out of immediate danger. After the first week Aunt Maud visited the hospital at least every other day. She arranged for the child's family to be brought to Nashville for the little girl's rehabilitation. She enrolled her in a private school and hired a tutor to work with her in the afternoons. Aunt Maud hired the child's uncle, Walter, to work in her garden, so that the family would have an income and not feel like beggars for receiving the money she gave them for the child's rehabilitation and education.

The next summer on Dave's second visit with Aunt Maud in Nashville, he asked her the name of the little girl that the train had hit the previous summer and whether she was all right. "Her name's Ruby. She's fine now. Course, she'll always have a little limp. But she's fine. She's smart, at least as smart as a colored child can be. You'll see her tomorrow. I'm going to bring her up here to the house to play with you."

And Dave and Ruby played together the next day and on many days that summer and on the summer that followed, but Aunt Maud put a stop to Ruby's visits when Dave turned eight, because it wouldn't do, she said, for a white boy to grow up playing with a little colored girl.

WHEN DAVID AND I entered the living room, Celia was sitting with my book open upside down on her lap. Her eyes were closed, and she was smiling. As she opened her eyes, she said, "It's a wonderful story, . . . *Gramps*. But I'm going to have to get used to saying *Gramps.*"

"You haven't told me how you met."

"How could we 'ave forgotten that? It was all because of you and Celia's grandmother. I went to that festival celebrating southern writers in Atlanta because they were reading one of your stories. You remember. It was last winter when you were sick with the flu and couldn't go. And Celia went because they were reading one of her grandmother's stories. We started talking about how much our grandparents' stories were alike; and we kept on talking . . . about lots and lots of other things, like we'd known each other before."

"So Ruby and I brought you two together."

"That's right. I still can't believe you actually knew my grandmother! How I wish she was still alive and could tell us what she thinks! Are we making a terrible mistake?"

"No! No! No! Ruby would tell you it's time. *It's about time*, that's exactly what she'd say. It was meant to be; I know people say that all the time, but now it's really true."

In spite of all I could do, I could not staunch the tears that flowed in streams down my cheeks. The curse visited to the third and fourth generations was broken. David and Celia rose holding hands with each other. David enveloped Celia and me together in a bear hug with his left arm, and

Celia gently brushed away the tears from my cheeks with her right hand while still holding David's right hand with her left hand. She continued to pat my face and move her fingertips under my eyes just as Ruby had done long ago when we'd said goodbye.

# A Private Friendship

T he memory of her first encounter with Lydia Trottling still caused Phyllis to feel a twinge of embarrassment and regret, nothing of course in comparison to how she felt about the things that happened over the last several months. She'd debated whether to take the stack of her back issues of *The New Yorker* and the *Saturday Evening Post* down to the colored school. A couple of times a year the town library discarded the books that were being replaced with new ones. Phyllis was in charge of the library volunteers, and she asked the other ladies to bring their old magazines to donate along with the tattered books. She had thought that the children at Booker T. Washington could cut photographs out of the magazines, but she'd been surprised that many of the parents also wanted to read the articles. Copies of the *Saturday Evening Post* and the *Readers Digest* might be of some interest to them, but she couldn't believe they would appreciate *The New Yorker*. Even so, Phyllis couldn't bear to throw them in the garbage and had taken a stack of them to the school.

"Do you know who that woman over there is . . . in the gray suit?" Phyllis had asked one of the library volunteers. She was better dressed and better groomed than any of the volunteers but so thin that Phyllis wondered if she were ill. She stood apart from both the white women volunteers and the parents of the students from Booker T. Washington.

"That's the wife of the colored doctor down at Lincoln Hospital."

In order to make conversation Phyllis had asked Lydia Trottling if she might be interested in reading *The New Yorker*. She'd meant it as a compliment or so she'd told herself. "I don't imagine anyone else would enjoy them," she'd added as a veiled indication of respect for her education and sophistication.

"Oh, I already subscribe to *The New Yorker*. I was just wondering who else might like them." Lydia had probably noticed Phyllis's flush of chagrin and glanced down at the issue in her hand to avert her eyes. "I especially enjoyed the poems in this one."

"W. H. Auden." Phyllis was relieved to recall what she'd read several months ago. "He's probably my favorite poet."

"Mine as well." Lydia's voice was as trim and well groomed as her hair. Only her hands fluttered with slight excitement, but even those movements were subdued and studied. "But I really like his poem in this month's *Atlantic* better."

"I don't get *The Atlantic Monthly*." Phyllis could feel her face flushing more deeply.

"I've almost finished with it. Would you like for me to pass it along?"

Phyllis felt her face turn deep crimson. "Very much. Thank you. That would be very kind."

LYDIA HAD BROUGHT THE copy of *The Atlantic Monthly* to Phyllis's home the next week. She had sat primly on the edge of the sofa, as if it would be an insult to lean back; and they'd discussed both of Auden's poems. Phyllis couldn't remember anyone else feeling about poetry and thinking as she did about Auden's work since she was in college. Lydia had asked if she would like to have her copies of *The Atlantic Monthly* every month. Phyllis had enthusiastically accepted the offer, as much to be able to talk with Lydia Trottling as to have the magazines. She had never before met an educated colored woman (or a black woman as she would say today, although it was difficult to imagine Lydia as being really black—her complexion was not as dark as some of Phyllis's friends who "lay out" in the sun all summer and her grammar and enunciation were impeccable). Phyllis had subscribed to *Harper's Bazaar,* in order to have something to contribute from her side as they swapped magazines and to have another reason to meet during the month and talk about the articles. And so their friendship had begun.

IF PHYLLIS KEPT THEIR friendship a secret it wasn't because she was ashamed of associating with a black woman (or so she told herself) but rather because she cherished their conversations like a hidden treasure that she didn't want to share with anyone else. In any case there was no one else in the town who would even understand what they talked about, much less would have felt the same kind of emotional attachment to poetry. Of course Emmalou, her sister-in-law, who snooped into all her business, once asked her, "Why does that Nigra doctor's wife come around to your house so regular?"

"We swap some magazines."

"I reckon it's right generous for you to give her your *literary* magazines." Emmalou's eyes opened up and her lips pursed with the word *literary*. "But looks like to me she could afford to buy her own magazines, being a doctor's wife and all, even if they are colored."

Phyllis wanted to tell Emmalou that Lydia Trottling was the most interesting, well-educated, sophisticated woman in town and was probably her closest friend; but she said nothing, because she couldn't have made Emmalou understand such sentiments, or so she told herself.

Every Friday since their husbands had died Phyllis and Emmalou had gone to lunch together. It had been Phyllis's main social outing before she met Lydia, and she still enjoyed it. Before the Grandview Restaurant was built they'd had to drive to Athens. Emmalou was good company. She wasn't a gossip, and she had a good heart. They talked mostly about family members and the old and sick people in the church. Phyllis had to admit that Emmalou was far more generous in helping people than she was—making casseroles, offering to drive people to the doctor, telephoning them before going to the grocery store to ask if they needed her to pick up something for them.

Phyllis had met Emmalou in college as a freshman, when Emmalou was a senior. When she graduated, Phyllis had accepted the job teaching English in the high school and was pleased to know someone in the "Teacherage," the old house converted into four apartments for the single female teachers. After the first couple of years as teachers came and went and moved in and moved out, Phyllis and Emmalou decided to share an apartment together. After another couple of years Emmalou married the older brother of the family that owned the town's cotton mill, although she continued to teach "home ec" until their first child was born. After another couple of years Phyllis married the younger brother of the cotton mill dynasty.

Despite being the wealthiest family in town, the brothers were often called "the poor McKay boys," because of the congenital heart problems that afflicted the male members of the family. Emmalou's husband died before they'd celebrated a dozen years of marriage, leaving her with two young girls. (Because they were females, they hadn't inherited the family curse.) Both of Emmalou's daughters lived in another state now with their own families and visited only a couple of times a year. Phyllis's husband made it to their twentieth wedding anniversary, but they'd decided not to have children so that the genetic illness would not be perpetuated, in case they would have conceived boys. Except for Emmalou and her family, that always included Phyllis in their visits and holidays, Phyllis was quite alone.

Both Phyllis and Emmalou were left "well fixed financially," as people in town often said. They continued to live in the big Georgian brick homes built side by side on Main Street and often talked about selling one of them or even both of them and moving into a smaller apartment as they'd lived together decades earlier in the "Teacherage."

In the end, inertia, memories associated with the belongings that filled the rambling rooms, and a lack of financial necessity coalesced to prevent their acting on any change in their living arrangements, to which a desire for privacy was added on Phyllis's side, although privacy would not have been an issue for Emmalou.

Even with the expenses of maintaining two large houses and each employing a cook and a cleaning woman, both Phyllis and Emmalou had large enough incomes to assist both civic endeavors and individual people in need. Phyllis was the principal patron of the town library; and Emmalou made up the shortfall in the expenses of the cannery, where families from out in the country and many people in town with gardens came to "put up food for the winter," as Emmalou said. She also bought several steers each fall that were slaughtered during canning season, ostensibly for her own use but actually primarily to give away as meat for vegetable stew mixtures along with a packet of herbs and spices of her own secret (and well-known to everyone) recipe.

The sisters-in-law joined their efforts in awarding college scholarships to deserving young people from the high school, and over the years they were proud of the graduations of twenty-seven of their recipients, who would not otherwise have gone to college, three of whom were black students from Booker T. Washington. Phyllis had hesitated about offering the black students scholarships when one of the teachers approached Emmalou. Phyllis was afraid of "opening up a can of worms and overextending ourselves"; but Emmalou insisted that "the colored schools need good teachers." Phyllis always tended to be more cautious and Emmalou more generous in their deliberations about benevolent contributions.

Their largest joint investment was bankrolling Cathy Webster's venture in opening the Grandview Restaurant. Cathy had been one of Emmalou's last home ec students and their only scholarship recipient to major in home ec in college. She was Emmanlou's star pupil, who had received blue ribbons in sewing and canning and cooking at the county fair. Phyllis noted that for her application Cathy also wrote the most polished essay that they'd ever received. Cathy and her husband Harry had scraped together a considerable amount of money from his wages as a truck driver and her teacher's salary, but they were far short of what was needed to launch Cathy's dream of opening a "first class restaurant." Emmalou observed that "they'd started from nothing, because both of their families were the po'est of the poor dirt farmers." Phyllis and Emmalou invested in the Grandview because they believed in Cathy and thought that they'd eventually receive a good return on their money, but they admitted to each other that they also selfishly wanted to be able to go out for a decent meal without having to drive almost thirty miles there and the same distance back.

Most of Cathy's dishes were good country cooking—steaks and fish and chicken—but were always fresh and well prepared. She sometimes experimented with more exotic food—her asparagus and snow peas medley had a light sauce with ingredients that defied even Emmalou's discerning palate, and her molten chocolate desert was beyond anything that Emmalou had ever taught or attempted to prepare. Although the lobby with its plush red velvet cushions "looked like a New Orleans madam's parlor" according to Phyllis's sniffed whisper that caused Emmalou to giggle, they were both proud of Cathy and her restaurant; and within ten years they'd received the full repayment of their loan with interest. Even after settling the balance of her debt in full, Cathy still insisted on listing Phyllis and Emmalou as "founders" along with Harry and herself on the little brass plaque beside the fountain in the lobby. Phyllis was simultaneously annoyed, amused, and flattered by having her name on the plaque. Emmalou was unconflictedly pleased to have her name inscribed.

MORE THAN A YEAR was required for Phyllis and Lydia to call each other by their first names, rather than Mrs. McKay and Mrs. Trottling. Another year passed before they spoke of anything in their personal lives. Their friendship was animated by the poetry that they entered into like a rarefied world unconnected to the town where they lived, a world apart from their family members and other friends.

Occasionally they began to speak to each other about their past experiences and other friends and family members. Phyllis usually elicited the information from Lydia as an extension of their discussions of poetry. Where Lydia first encountered W. H. Auden and T. S. Eliot and e e cummings and Stephen Spender led to revelations of her college years; Phyllis had not even known where Lydia went to college (Tuskegee Institute). Then Phyllis talked about her English courses at GSCW (Georgia State College for Women). Phyllis asked if Lydia had any family members who were also interested in modern literature, and Lydia said that neither of her two sisters nor her brother had any such interest nor did her husband nor did any of her friends from college, to her great regret. Phyllis had not even known that Lydia had siblings and revealed her sadness at being an only child. Neither of them articulated their sorrow at being childless.

One afternoon in April Phyllis stopped at Lydia's house to deliver a magazine and continue their discussion of T. S. Eliot's *Wasteland*. Since the poem began "April is the cruelest month," they'd decided to trace down all the allusions and foreign phrases during the month and had divided them up like members of a college study group preparing for a final examination. Phyllis had just returned from lunch with Emmalou at the Grandview and asked Lydia rather casually, "Have you ever gotten take-out from the Grandview? We like Cathy's fried chicken warmed up for supper and usually get a few pieces to take home after we have lunch there."

Phyllis thought she knew Lydia well enough to mention "take-out" without embarrassing her by an explicit reference to her being banned from the Grandview dining room. (There was a window on the side of the restaurant where food was sold to black people and even to white people who were uncomfortable sitting at the tables inside or were improperly dressed or were in a hurry.)

Lydia's face darkened. Phyllis had never before seen such an expression or such a color around her eyes and on her cheeks.

"No indeed. I can fry up my own chicken. If I were going to stand in line like a beggar in a souk, it would have to be for something special. Not fried chicken or snap beans cooked to mush with fatback."

"We just do it to save time. Emmalou's dishes are much better prepared than anything we can get there." Phyllis babbled on in a vain attempt to cover her chagrin. "I just thought . . . I wasn't thinking. I'm sorry I mentioned it."

A dam seemed to burst in Lydia, and she spoke to Phyllis as she'd never spoken before. "You have no idea what it's like to be well-dressed and have money in your purse and have to drive hundreds of miles without a decent place to stop and eat, maybe a thousand miles in between places to spend the night, if you want to make a trip to see your sister. You're driving a brand new car, but there's not even a clean place to use the bathroom on your journey, nor any place at all for that matter."

"No, I really can't imagine. Emmalou and I used to complain about having to drive to Athens for lunch, and that's nothing. I never thought about it like that. I'm so sorry. I didn't mean . . ."

"Of course you didn't. Why would you have ever thought about it? I guess you just touched a nerve, and it unleashed . . . all that barrage. It's not your fault. I do apologize." Lydia began opening her copy of T. S. Eliot's complete poems that each of them had bought for their "little seminars," as they called them. "Here. We better get down to our study."

THE GRANDVIEW RESTAURANT WAS not mentioned again until September when Lydia called Phyllis one morning. It was unusual for them to speak on the telephone. They arranged their meetings from one time to the next and called only if one of them was ill or needed to cancel for some other reason. "Phyllis, I thought you should know that some people are planning a sit-in demonstration at the Grandview Restaurant in the next couple of weeks. Most of them are young people from the community college. I believe there will be some white students with them. A few local leaders from the black community are planning to join them. I intend to participate. I thought you should know."

"Lydia! I can't imagine you demonstrating." The newspaper images of people sitting in doorways and being carried away by police flipped through Phyllis's mind, and she really couldn't imagine her tall, thin, sophisticated, always impeccably dressed, well-groomed friend involved in such a scene.

"I know. I couldn't imagine it myself until recently. But I decided it was just time. It's time to take a stand. I believe there will be some prominent older white people involved, a couple of Civil Rights leaders from the University of Georgia in Athens. No local white people that I'm aware of."

Phyllis could hear between Lydia's words the request, not a plea, more like a dare, as they might have dared each other as young girls to do something brave and risky—*won't you join us?* But Phyllis couldn't conceive of doing such a thing, not anywhere, certainly not here in this town, not at the Grandview, not to Cathy. "When will all this take place?" Phyllis didn't want to imply that she might consider joining them. She hoped Lydia understood that she asked in order to be sure to avoid arriving unawares at the Grandview in the midst of the demonstration.

"They haven't set a firm date. Sometime soon. Probably within the next couple of weeks."

"I appreciate your letting me know."

"I thought you should be aware . . ." Lydia's voice had changed. The request, the dare, had fled from between and below her words. "I imagine your sister-in-law would have a hard time with it." Now Phyllis knew that Lydia was speaking to disguise her original intention, to allay her disappointment in Phyllis's response and lack of understanding, to cover her deep feelings with the proper etiquette that was their common and familiar discourse.

PERHAPS BECAUSE PHYLLIS WANTED to suppress her feelings of guilt and confusion, she had forgotten her conversation with Lydia about a potential demonstration at the Grandview when Emmalou called to confirm their customary lunch on Friday. They were seated at one of the few tables with a view of the parking lot. Emmalou's back was against the window, but Phyllis saw three cars pull in together with three or four black people and two white people in each car. Every word from Lydia's telephone conversation rushed back into her mind within seconds, like a movie that suddenly flashes forward.

"What do you all want?" Phyllis could hear the shrill anger and fear in Cathy's voice and was grateful that Emmalou's partial deafness prevented her from making out the precise words from the raised voices.

"We would like to have lunch." One of the young white men spoke for the group, although he appeared somewhat older than the others—perhaps he was a graduate student.

"You can get take-out at the side."

"We would like to be served in the dining room."

"We don't serve mixed groups at the Grandview." Cathy's throat had become constricted with contempt and indignation.

"We would be agreeable to sitting at separate tables." Lydia's words were as soft and genteel and precise as ever. Phyllis didn't think Lydia had yet seen her seated in the dining room. The young white man who had been the group's spokesman gave Lydia a censoring glance, as if she'd committed some indiscreet *faux pas.*

Now Cathy shrieked like a woman who was being assaulted and reverted to her words and grammar from long ago in the country. "We don't serve no Niggers in here."

"You have to serve people regardless of their race. It's the law." The young white man spoke his memorized words as if he'd rehearsed them for a play.

"We're closed. We're not serving any more meals for lunch."

"What time are you opening for dinner?"

"We're not going to be open tonight."

"Mrs. Webster, we'll keep coming back every day, day after day until . . ." Lydia spoke again and once again was interrupted by another white college student.

"Come on. Let's sit down at the tables."

"I'm calling the po-lice!"

"You do that. You're the one breaking the law. We'll see you in court." The older graduate student spoke again.

"What's going on?" Emmalou was rarely distracted from her food by raised voices, and some of the businessmen who ate lunch at the Grandview often talked and laughed boisterously.

"I don't know. There's some sort of hullabaloo about someone's check, I guess. Emmalou, you finished?" Phyllis was relieved that Emmalou had for once cleaned her plate and would not be calling for a doggy bag. "We can slip out the side door and avoid the congestion in the lobby."

"We haven't paid our bill yet."

"I paid on the way in." Phyllis knew that she could pay Cathy later and avoid embarrassing her.

"That's peculiar."

"Come on. It's time to leave." Phyllis was even more startled by her own commanding tone than was Emmalou, who raised her eyebrows and opened her lips in gaping disbelief.

As they stood to leave, Lydia Trottling saw them; and she and Phyllis looked at each other. Phyllis nodded to Lydia. Lydia didn't acknowledge her but smiled sadly as one smiles at a child who is misbehaving. Phyllis wondered why she felt guilty before Lydia's smile. She was doing nothing wrong. She wasn't the one who had broken the law or crossed the line of long-accepted custom.

Phyllis and Emmalou had almost reached Phyllis's car when Harry Webster's pickup truck came speeding into the parking lot, throwing up gravel. As Harry entered the restaurant even Emmalou could hear his screaming voice, swearing with more rage and hysteria than Cathy's. "You goddamned stinking Niggers. You cock-sucking bitches. You lily-livered Nigger-loving sons of bitches . . ."

"I'm not as gullible and naïve as you think I am, Phyllis," Emmalou said as she closed her door on the passenger's side of the car. "I know very well what's going on."

PHYLLIS WAS SHOPPING FOR groceries the afternoon that Cathy came to tell them about closing their restaurant, but Emmalou repeated her words almost verbatim. "They closed the restaurant that very afternoon. Just bolted the door and put up a closed sign. And it's been shut up ever since. Cathy and Harry are trying to sell the whole she-bang. You can't blame them."

Phyllis sat in silence as Emmalou continued. "I feel so sorry for Cathy. She was so proud of the Grandview. We all were. You know how big lawyers and doctors and professors had taken to coming over from Athens for the Sunday brunch. It was getting quite a reputation. Cathy told me it was just like being raped. She felt like that girl from the mill village that got raped in the high school gym. Cathy still doesn't feel like facing people. She said she won't even drive by there on the highway any more. She says she still trembles so bad she can't drive the car, just like it was going back to a place like somewhere she'd been raped." Emmalou's cheeks quivered when she mentioned rape, as they'd always done when she talked about sexual things.

"Cathy told me the sheriff dragged them out like drunks being thrown out of some cheap roadhouse—the kind of place she said her father would never even let her get near. Why would any decent, self-respecting white person come down here and get mixed up with Niggers like that?" Phyllis opened her mouth with shock. She'd never heard Emmalou pronounce the word without a terminal "a" before that moment. "It ruined everything. Cathy thinks she's ruined for life. Of course she's not. She'll recover. It's gonna be a real hardship on us, too, you know. We'll really miss having a nice place to eat in town any more, but of course we'll manage a lot better than Cathy, poor thing."

"Maybe someone will buy the restaurant and open it back up," Phyllis ventured in an attempt to end Emmalou's diatribe.

"They'd have to serve *them*. You think I'd sit down there and eat with Nigras? How could they destroy something nice and beautiful like that? How could any respectable person refuse to leave when they were asked nicely, when they were told everything was closed?"

Phyllis thought of dozens of responses, but she remained silent because she had not yet formed coherent thoughts within her mind, nevertheless thoughts that could be articulated as words in her mouth.

*The Atlanta Constitution* CARRIED the story on the front page about a member of a prominent Hale County Georgia family who was arrested at the Governor's Mansion with a group of young black and white Civil Rights demonstrators. Phyllis was pictured sitting on the sidewalk in front of the gate. Her full pleated skirt, which she'd chosen because she knew she couldn't sit down on the ground in a tight shirt, was spread around her like an open umbrella, as if she'd been a cheerleader who had spun and dropped into place after rallying the high school football fans. That afternoon *The Atlanta Journal* published a slightly rewritten story on the very front page and in its continuation on page eight pictured Phyllis in jail holding the bars on each side of her shoulders and looking utterly bewildered. Her always perfectly shaped coiffure bloused out around her ears as if she'd just gotten out of bed and forgotten to brush it.

As she'd planned to do, Phyllis had spent the night in the Fulton County jail, but the next morning she'd called the Atlanta lawyer who had helped to settle her husband's estate, and he'd sent a member of his firm to pay her fine and have her released. She would not have to make any other court appearances. It was all over.

EMMALOU CALLED PHYLLIS TO tell her that she was coming over to see her—it was unusual for her to call; she usually just dropped by. Then Emmalou walked down the long brick path from her front door to the sidewalk and up the long concrete path from the sidewalk to Phyllis's front door rather than going the short distance across their back lawns from her kitchen door to Phyllis's kitchen door—it was the first time she had ever taken such a route in all the decades they'd lived next door to each other.

"Come in, Emmalou. I take it you've seen the papers."

"I read about it in *The Journal*." Emmalou subscribed to the afternoon newspaper. "Then I went downtown and bought *The Constitution*, but it didn't tell me much that I didn't already know."

"Come on in and sit down." Since they were in the front part of the house, they went into the parlor. That, too, was unusual.

"What on earth possessed you? I think you must have been out of your mind."

"It was just something I felt I had to do."

"Well, I suppose that colored doctor's wife you're so friendly with had something to do with it."

"My friendship with Lydia certainly made me think about it. The things she told me . . . they just started gnawing inside me until I felt I had to do something; but Lydia didn't know anything about my trip to Atlanta."

"It would sure have been a whole lot easier if you'd just joined that gang that went to the Grandview. That's what I would have done."

"I know that's what you'd have done, Emmalou. You're a whole lot bolder than I am. I'm more of a coward than you are. And I just couldn't do that to Cathy . . . and the people here in town."

"Not that I would of gone to either place, of course. I think Lester Mattox is a perfect fool; but still, Phyllis, how could you have done such a thing? I think you must be sick. I think maybe you've lost your mind."

"Maybe so."

They were quiet for a while and both of them watched the little round gold balls go back and forth and quietly tick in the glass case underneath the dial of the clock from Austria. Phyllis felt the dark green velvet upholstery of the sofa with her fingertips and remembered the hard, cold steel on the sides of the cot in the jail.

"Phyllis, does that woman mean that much to you, that you would go and do something like that for her?"

"I told you, Emmalou. I didn't do it for her. I did it for myself. But, yes. Our poetry discussions meant a lot to me. You say I've lost my mind, but sometimes I think meeting with Lydia may have saved my sanity."

"I just can't understand it. I don't understand it one little bit, but I suppose you and that colored woman will be even friendlier now. I reckon she's real proud of you."

"I don't know. I can't even guess how Lydia would react. We won't be having our poetry discussion any more, I suspect. I won't be seeing Lydia as often any more. Of course, we'll meet up from time to time. But I'll miss it. I'll miss her. I'll miss it dreadfully."

"Why on earth not! After all you went and did. She ought to be grateful. She ought to give you credit."

"That's not how it works. The world we were escaping from has been smashed . . . demolished; and so our private little world is gone, too."

"Well, Phyllis, I simply cannot fathom all this. I still think you've lost your senses."

"Maybe I have, Emmalou. Lots of things don't make very good sense to me right now."

"Well, I guess we'll be seeing a lot more of one another. You're not gonna do a lot of socializing with folks in town for a while, more than a polite, civil little *howdy do*. I'm the only one you got now."

"And you don't know how much that means to me, Emmalou." Phyllis felt the tears forming in her eyes.

"Oh, stop blubbering. You know you can always count on me."

"I appreciate that more than you'll ever know."

Emmalou smiled. "I know plenty. I know a whole heap more than you think I do."

# Lazarus, Come Forth

The parish cemetery rolled down the steep hillside below the church, and the gravestones on the terraces reminded me of sheep on the Scottish moors north of Edinburgh where I'd studied for a year after finishing seminary. The teak bench beside my predecessor's grave was my favorite place to sit for lunch on rare days when I wasn't rushing from the office to the hospital or to the town hall for an invocation or to a hearing involving one of our outreach ministries or on days like today when I was pondering a troubling issue.

The Rev. Robert Wardlaw, buried here, had died over a decade before I was called to be Rector of St. Mary and St. Martha's Church three years ago. I wondered, as I often did, why Lazarus was omitted from the church named for his sisters. Especially today I wondered, although I could imagine the reasons for neglecting him.

In the winter and early spring I could see the river at the bottom of the hill. Now, in the late afternoon after returning from my encounter with Holly at Bethany Mills, with trees along the riverbank in full leaf, there were only occasional glimpses of water when the sun hit at just the right angle to shoot a reflected shaft of light through the green branches like stars twinkling in the night sky. The church had also probably been visible from this spot when it was first built, but now the trees had grown up at the top of the hill to hide the church as they had grown at the bottom to obscure the river.

Today was not one of the rare leisurely days when I was able to come here for lunch to munch my sandwich and sip coffee from my thermos as I gazed down the hillside toward the river. Today I was driven here by the most serious crisis of my ministry, perhaps the most threatening catastrophe of my life. Today I wondered if my vocation as a priest was over. Today I wondered if the meaning and relevance of my life were coming to an end or whether like the brother of Mary and Martha, who had been forgotten in this place, I might be restored to life.

When the bishop called me last week, I'd guessed why he wanted to meet with me. As I'd entered his office yesterday, his expression brought a momentary twinge of alarm—I knew it would be a messy, aggravating business—but from the moment he opened his mouth and began to speak, each of his words slew a spiritual cell within me until in the end I was a dead man inside my physical body.

JACK HINSON HAD ARRIVED at St. Mary and St. Martha's Church to great acclaim and even greater expectation by the parish. He'd graduated *cum laude* from seminary at Yale and then studied for a year at the University of Edinburgh in Scotland. Then he'd served a four-year curacy at one of the most prestigious parishes in New York City. The most oft repeated exclamations exchanged among the members were: "I don't know how we got him to come here!" "He's just perfect!" "He'll do wonderful things for our church!"

Before the first month had passed several matrons of the church joined by other females in their social clique began plotting a match between Jack and Holly Gilbert, who was perhaps a year or so older than Jack; but their approximate same ages made them seem to be the perfect couple for a romantic pairing.

The Gilberts represented the old aristocracy of the town, cradle Episcopalians, wealthy, generous contributors to the church and all local charities, genteel, charming, and beloved by everyone. It was said, with considerable truth, that Harry and Sally Gilbert were the only people in Bithynia who never had an enemy.

The town had been shocked when Holly, their only child, became pregnant during her senior year of high school. In keeping with the family's values and principles, a marriage was quickly arranged for Holly and almost as quickly dissolved after she gave birth to Henry, named for his grandfather.

In high school Holly had been a ravishing beauty with auburn hair, big blue eyes, and a perfect complexion; and she was still probably the most strikingly good-looking woman in town. If she wasn't ever the top of her class academically, her grades were acceptable in high school; and she was president of virtually every student organization.

HARRY AND SALLY REARED their grandson during his infant years so that Holly could attend a branch campus of the state university, where her grades were still passable, although she didn't participate in any extracurricular activities so that she could spend every weekend with her baby boy.

Jack was invited as a guest to four dinner parties where Holly was also a guest during his first month in Bithynia; and he received many hints bordering on explicit suggestions and leaning toward ultimatums that he ask Holly for a date, an idea to which he was in no way averse.

Jack was dazzled and besotted after the first hour of their first date. He had never met a woman who touched him with her fingertips and also tempted him to touch her while still maintaining clear boundaries of sensual propriety. He had chosen to drive into Atlanta for dinner, both to preserve their privacy and also to have time to talk in the car on the way down and back and really get to know Holly personally away from the groups where she behaved with the perfectly gracious etiquette and with the sensitive responsiveness in which she had been trained and groomed all her life.

Holly seemed able to converse about any subject. (Later Jack realized that she was adept at seeming to listen with interest to any subject being discussed without ever contributing much herself.)

On their second date Jack took Holly to a foreign film festival that was showing classics from France and Sweden. He especially wanted her to see an Ingmar Bergman movie that had been an emotional epiphany for him during college. Holly seemed distracted throughout the movie, looking at her nails, gazing around the audience, finally closing her eyes. Jack apologized for exposing her to Bergman without any preparation or warning. "It's petty heavy stuff. I know it can be disturbing."

"Oh, it's not that. I just don't much care for movies that aren't in Technicolor."

On their third date Holly talked endlessly and nonstop about the personal conflicts between people at Bethany Mills. She was the office manager at the company founded by her great-grandfather. By all reports Holly was efficient and effective at her job. Jack gathered from her monologue that her relationships with people in the office were a major part of her life. He told her that she must be proud to be involved in the production of high quality hosiery and women's nightgowns and undergarments.

"Oh, I've never worn those things. They're just for the common people, you know."

On their fourth date Holly described for almost two hours her difficulty in finding a beautician who could properly cut and add highlights to her hair after the stylist she had used since high school moved to Atlanta. "I've tried eleven salons. Eleven, Jack! Can you imagine?" She appeared to be on the brink of tears, and Jack was utterly befuddled about what to say or do to comfort her obvious distress.

And on their fifth date Jack attempted to extricate himself from any further expectation that he was courting Holly. He had thought long and hard about just what to say to her—he knew how much hope some women in the church had invested in their incipient romance and how their disappointment might adversely affect his ministry. He had lost several hours of sleep for a couple of nights trying to choose the right words.

Jack took Holly to the nicest restaurant in town and deliberately made an eight o'clock reservation after inventing an excuse for the late hour, so that by the time they would have finished dessert and coffee, few, if any, other diners would be left to overhear and observe them.

"Holly, you can't imagine how much I admire you. I've really enjoyed our dates and getting to know you. I think you're the most beautiful woman I ever met, certainly the most gorgeous woman I ever dated; but I don't think we have enough common interests to pursue a serious relationship. I'm still dazzled by you, and I really, really wanted it to work; but . . ."

"Oh, Jack, you flatter me. Quite frankly, I didn't experience any bells and banjos either. I hope we can still be friends—isn't that supposed to be the man's line?" She laughed with the warm, mellow voice that was, like her face and body, perfect and alluring; and Jack wondered again if perhaps he was making a huge mistake and was missing something. How could a woman so beautiful and so able to respond appropriately with perfect etiquette to any situation not be a rare "catch" and an ideal minister's wife? But he knew better. He had tried to find something more in Holly below the surface.

JACK PLAYED GOLF WITH Al Benson almost every Saturday afternoon. Al was the only other eligible bachelor in town who had passed his third decade of life. Al was good company and undemanding, and Jack didn't have to consider marrying him or suffering the community's hostility if he ever broke off their friendship even after several months of regular Saturday outings. Al was an easy conversationalist, and Jack made the enormous mistake of telling Al that he had to stop dating Holly because "she was as shallow as the babies' wading pool at the country club" without realizing that Al was the biggest male gossip in town. Soon the quip about Holly had spread to every nook and cranny of their local polite society.

WHEN HOLLY CALLED AND asked if she could arrange an appointment with him at the church in his office, Jack panicked. His secretary, Miss Madge Ethridge, had warned him after the gossip from his quip about Holly had become common currency in town, as she blinked at him with magnified eyes through her big round tri-focal spectacles and wrinkled her brow and pursed her lips and touched at the hair around her ears, "You watch out for that Holly Gilbert, Pastor, she always gets her revenge, even if she has to wait a long time." Jack had been bemused then at how Madge, a staunch Presbyterian, always called him "pastor" rather than "father"; but at that moment her words rang alarm bells in his mind.

"Of course, Holly, I'd be delighted to see you. How's four thirty on Thursday after you leave the office?"

JACK'S LEFT HAND QUIVERED under his desk after Holly sat down opposite him, but she never mentioned herself and gave no indication that she had heard about his inconsiderate gaffe. If he had thought, he would have realized that Holly would never mention the insult or confront him directly, even if she had overheard it. She would demonstrate the same placid and cordial demeanor whether or not his remark had gotten back to her.

Holly's concern was her son, Henry. "He's fourteen now, and he's never had a male role model. Daddy did what he could to fill in as a father, but he's old . . . and old fashioned, as you know." She chuckled in her warm, mellow voice.

"I hope you don't want me to give him a lesson about the birds and the bees. I'm not really . . ."

"Oh, no. Henry knows all about sex, like most boys nowadays, I guess. Just talk to him. See if you can figure out what's going on in his pretty little head." She chuckled again. "Boys stop communicating with their mothers at his age, and there's no one else . . ."

"I'll give it a try. No promises." Jack had always found young adolescents a mystery, like aliens from another planet. Even when leading a church youth group during seminary and at his parish in New York, he never knew what to say to them.

"Oh, I'd be so grateful to you, Jack! I think you'll be perfect. Would it be convenient for him to come by early next week one day after school?"

Jack pretended to scan his appointment book, although he knew his schedule without reading it. "Tuesday or Wednesday afternoon?"

"Tuesday would be better. He has drama club on Wednesdays."

HENRY GILBERT II WAS a pale imitation of his mother. His grandfather had adopted him before he was two years old, so that he would have the Gilbert name, with his father's enthusiastic consent after the old man made a generous donation to his former son-in-law's bank account. His thick wavy hair tended more toward red than his mother's auburn locks, and his eyes were also a lighter shade of blue. He was handsome, almost too pretty for a boy; but he was not strikingly beautiful like Holly.

Jack found Henry remarkably easy to talk to, unlike other boys his age. Henry had been tutored in the art of polite conversation like his mother, by his mother. He was able to respond and converse easily and endlessly, like Holly, without ever really saying anything or revealing anything about himself.

"Do you ever see your father?" Jack decided to try a bold frontal query to break through Henry's composure during their second appointment. They had agreed to meet every Tuesday afternoon for a few weeks.

"He comes around once or twice every year. I think my mother and grandfather arrange it. He never seems very interested in seeing me."

"How do you feel about him?"

Henry shrugged. "I don't feel much one way or the other about him."

"I guess your grandfather has been more like a father to you."

Henry glared directly at Jack as if he were flashing a bolt of electricity toward Jack from his pale blue eyes. Jack had hit a nerve at last inside the boy. "He tries to make me perfect. I hate having to be perfect for him."

Henry paused, and Jack gave him a few moments to continue, but he remained silent. "What do you mean by *being perfect*?" Jack prodded; but Henry had retreated back into the polite, conditioned behavior in which he had been well groomed and trained.

"Awh, I shouldn't have said that. My grandfather's a wonderful man. He's been great to me. He's just from a different generation, as Mom says."

During the following weeks Jack became increasingly empathetic with Henry's veiled discomfort. Although he was supposed to have the bishop's permission for counseling beyond six sessions, he didn't think of his visits with Henry as counseling; and when Miss Ethridge had to schedule a series of dental appointments on Tuesday afternoons, he ignored the diocesan policy of not being alone with teenagers unless another adult was present. Jack thought that insurance liability issues were controlling the world, and he rebelled against their dominance of the church.

Henry often expressed more in smiles and revealed more in glances than in words, but occasional verbal outbursts would crack his controlled exterior. When Jack asked him about his grandmother, Henry almost snarled. "All she's interested in is correct grammar and good manners. Underneath she wishes I'd never been born."

When Jack asked Henry about friends, his face crumpled. "I don't have any friends, except maybe for you. Would it be all right if I called you *Jack*?"

Although Jack was uncomfortable with the suggestion, he didn't believe it was the moment to deny Henry's request. "Of course you may."

One Tuesday Henry seemed especially troubled and withdrawn. Jack prattled on about forthcoming events in the church and in town hoping that Henry would warm up and begin to talk. Finally, Jack hushed and left a silence between them that felt comfortable, even intimate and consoling. Henry began to relax.

"Can I tell you something, Jack?"

"Of course."

"It has to be confidential. You can't tell anyone. Especially not my grandfather. Not even Mom."

"Anything you tell me is confidential. Always."

"I like to be around boys better than girls."

Jack paused. He realized that this was dangerous territory. He wanted to choose his words wisely. "That's not unusual for boys your age. I felt about the same way when I was your age."

"I don't think it's my age. I think I may be gay. If my grandfather ever heard me say that, he'd kill me. Do you hate me for saying that?"

"Of course not." Jack felt a deep affection for Henry and sympathy for his situation.

"I don't know what I'll do when I graduate from high school and go away to college."

"You have to be who you are and live with integrity, but at fourteen you don't have to figure out the rest of your life."

"Have you ever been attracted to men, Jack?"

Jack wanted to be honest, but he wanted even more to be cautious and helpful to Henry. "I think everyone is attracted to both men and women at times in our lives. It doesn't have to be a sexual thing."

"Thanks, Jack. That really makes me feel better." Henry's smile was faint but genuine. As Henry rose to leave the office, Jack impetuously and foolishly got up and came around his desk and gave Henry a hug. He was startled to feel Henry's hand move down to his crotch. Jack gently pushed Henry's hand away.

"Don't you like me, Jack?"

"That's not appropriate, Henry. We've got to talk about the terms of how we get together from now on."

"JACK, HOW COULD YOU have been so stupid?" Sitting across the desk from the bishop I suddenly wondered how Henry had felt sitting across the desk from me. I wondered if I could show as much poise and composure as the fourteen year old boy had exhibited, but surely he hadn't felt as though life was slowly draining from his soul. "You broke every rule in the policy book. You didn't get permission or have consultation for sessions beyond six times . . ."

"I didn't think of it as counseling."

"Well you should have. And you didn't have another adult nearby . . ."

"I'm truly sorry about that. It was a mistake. It was stupid."

"It certainly was. I'm not sure I can save you."

*Jesus will save me; I just want you stand up for me*, I almost said it aloud but was able to suppress it. My old bishop would have protected his clergy first when they hadn't done anything wrong. This one guarded the institution first. Perhaps that's the way things worked now. "What can I do? I'll do whatever you advise, whatever you tell me to do."

"This is a nightmare. I hope we can keep it from going to the ecclesiastical court. God forbid its getting out to the civil authorities. With all that's been happening to the Romans, the press would have a field day."

"I know. I've been very foolish."

"Stupid. Stupid. There's no substance to this, is there? Be perfectly honest with me."

"No, sir. None whatsoever."

"Well, that's something. Phil Brown has been your spiritual director, hasn't he?"

"Yes, sir."

"I want you to see him, and I want your permission for me to send your statement to him as well as the complaint."

"Of course. Could I read the complaint?"

"Not until we see where this is going, if it's going to our court or to the civil authorities, God forbid."

"I'll call Father Brown as soon as I get home."

"Sooner. Call him right now."

Father Phillip Brown suggested that we meet at his church as soon as possible, and I agreed. So we scheduled on appointment for the next morning.

"YOU'VE GOTTEN YOURSELF IN quite a pickle, laddie." Phil Brown's affected English accent seemed natural on his lips. He could have retired several years ago, but he kept on working because the priesthood was the only thing he knew how to do. He was a recovering alcoholic; and he reeked of tobacco, even on those rare occasions when he wasn't smoking his pipe or a cigarette.

"I need your help, counsel, absolution, whatever you can give me."

"I'll give you all I've got. I hope it'll be enough. I'll hear your confession later, but first tell me exactly what happened, and don't spare any details."

I related as completely and as accurately as I could recall the sessions with Henry, especially the final one, without betraying his confidence.

"I see. I see. And he touched you first?"

"I never touched him at all, except to move his hand away."

"The complaint says you hugged him first."

"That's true. It was a mistake. We'd had an emotional session. I just wanted to reassure him."

"Oh, Jesus." On Phil's lips the words were not taking the divine name in vain but rather a prayer of intercession. "I'm sure Bishop Ed reminded you that violated the policy guidelines."

I nodded solemnly.

"The complaint says you told him people can be attracted to both men and women."

I felt myself flushing deeply from my forehead to my throat. "I suppose that's an accurate statement. I didn't mean it had to be sexually . . ."

"Oh, Jesus, Jesus. You're in a real mess, Jack. Did you also tell him that you were attracted to both men and women?"

"That's out of context. I was trying to reassure him. I can't violate his confidence and tell you what he said to justify myself."

"Good man. But it may cost you. Dearly. Were you attracted to the boy?"

"Yes . . . no . . . I don't know quite what you mean. I was fond of him. I found him attractive. I was attracted by his good looks, as I'd been attracted by his mother's. And I'm so plain and homely. They're both uncommonly beautiful people, you know."

"Oh, Jesus, Jesus, Jesus. What about his mother? You dated her and broke up with her, didn't you?"

"How did you find out about that? Do you know Holly?"

"Everyone is this part of the state knows the Gilberts and has heard the gossip about Holly. She's bad news from way back."

For the first time it occurred to me that Holly might have prompted Henry to lure me into a trap. Could anyone be that cynical, that sinister? "Do you think Holly is behind all this—out of revenge?" Madge Ethridge's warning popped into my head again.

"With the Gilberts anything's possible, anything at all." Father Phil took off his horn rimmed spectacles and rubbed his eyes.

"What's going to happen to me, Father Phil?"

"Best case scenario, you'll be moved to another parish. Worst case, you'll land in jail."

"What if I'm defrocked?"

"Life goes on whether you're a priest or not."

"I never wanted to be anything but a priest. I'd rather go to prison. Surely you can understand that. The priesthood is my life just as life is the priesthood for you."

"Life and the priesthood are more than the Church."

"What can I do? What should I do?"

"Admit you're powerless to control the events you've set in motion. You can't manage them or their outcome. Turn your life over to God through our Lord Jesus Christ and the Holy Spirit, and seek God's will and the power to carry it out. Make amends to those you've hurt." Father Phil used the language of Alcoholics Anonymous but adapted it with more Trinitarian terminology in his spiritual direction. "Whether related to this situation or not, make amends wherever you can, to whomever you can. Then hold your head up and move on, and let the chips fall where they may. Are you ready to make your confession? After you've made your confession I may have something more to say to you."

BY THE TIME I drove back into town after my meeting with Father Phil, the whistle was blowing at Bethany Mills and workers were streaming out of the plant. I knew that Holly would still be at the office along with some other members of the staff, so I went straight to the visitors' parking lot and entered the building to find her. She was in the outer office, not her private quarters. "Holly, would you ask a couple of the ladies to stay around a few minutes and let me talk with you privately in your office? I'm not supposed to talk with you alone."

"I'm not supposed to talk to you at all."

"Holly, please. *Please*. I'll take just a few minutes."

Something in my voice and face must have melted Holly's intransigence. "Well, I suppose . . . Come on. Gladys, will you and Judy hang around for a few minutes? I need to ask you something after Father Jack leaves. He'll be just a few minutes."

Holly closed the half glass door, so that we could still be seen but not heard—I was glad that I didn't have to request that gesture for our privacy. "I'm sorry, Holly. I'm so very sorry for some things I said about you. You are the most beautiful woman I've ever dated, probably the most beautiful woman I've ever known. I was such a nerd in high school and even in college, and girls like you made fun of me. Maybe I was getting back at them—I don't know—but that's no excuse. I so wanted things to work out between us; and when they didn't . . . I guess I tried to blame you . . . just because we are different. I apologize. I said you were shallow . . ."

"As shallow as the baby pool at the club, I heard . . ."

"Yes." The rushing heat on my face reminded me of the blush I'd felt talking to Father Phil during an even more embarrassing confession. "I'm really sorry. Whatever happens I just wanted to clear my conscience and apologize to you."

"I see. And are you going to apologize to Henry, too?"

At first I didn't know what to say. "No, I don't have anything to apologize to Henry for. I didn't do anything wrong. I may not have always spoken wisely. Above all, I'm sorry I couldn't help him; and I'll say to you how sorry I am I couldn't do more for him, but I don't have anything to tell him I'm sorry for."

"I see. Is that all?"

If only I could read beneath Holly's placid, composed face to see what she was really thinking and feeling. "That's it."

AFTER VISITING HOLLY AT the mill and sitting on the bench looking down at the river until the sun had set, Jack tossed and turned all night thinking back over the times when he'd heard accusations of sexual misbehavior discussed or made against a priest.

Charges of sexual misconduct were only words in policy manuals and abstract ideas discussed in seminars for Jack until now. During his years in seminary and his study in Scotland he had heard about priests who had gotten into trouble and had been accused of wrongdoing after they had crossed boundaries of sexual propriety. The training that the diocese required all the clergy members to attend made him drowsy.

For the first time in years he recalled a memory from his childhood. Jack had admired Miss Leticia Ingram more than any woman in the world besides his mother. Miss Lettie had supervised Christian education and directed the junior choir at his church. Both of Jack's grandmothers had died before he was born, and he had pretended that Miss Lettie was his grandmother on Sunday mornings as she anchored the alto section of the adult choir and her deep voice rumbled below the shrill sounds above it like a river current conveying the meaning and continuity and flow of life. Whether she was speaking or singing, Miss Lettie's voice gave assurance and stability and endurance like the big organ pipes played by the pedals that resounded deeply and shook the building.

After the rumor spread around town that a child had burst into the parish office and had seen the priest bending down and kissing Miss Lettie on her lips, she had left the church within a few days and moved away within a few weeks; and the priest had been transferred to another parish a few months later.

THE VENETIAN BLINDS WERE not yet tinged with gray by the emerging light when I awoke and dressed after a few hours of fitful sleep. Outside the Rectory all was darkness, blackness. The engine of my car groaned reluctantly. The sun was just shooting rays of red and purple over the horizon as I headed north on the interstate highway with the South Carolina map on the passenger's seat beside me. I was wearing my clerical collar, my pass to get through almost any barrier, my ticket to enter almost any inner sanctum.

Although I'd never seen this nursing home, it had the appearance and especially the familiar scent of other nursing homes. I sought out one of the black attendants because they were usually more helpful and responsive than the nurses. A large black woman smiled at me. The other women at the nurses' station frowned over their sheaths of charts and schedules and never looked up. "I'd like to visit Miss Leticia Ingram . . . I'm sorry I don't remember her married name. I knew her a long time ago." And I prevaricated, "I happen to be in the area."

It was mid afternoon. Perhaps she was napping. At least it was early enough not to interfere with a noon lunch or a five o'clock supper, the two important events of the day in most nursing homes.

"You mean our dear, sweet Miz Jones. She be our pet. I know she gonna love to see you. She don't miss nothin'. Jus' you follow me."

Down the central hall, then left, then right—by habit I memorized the route, even though I would probably never trace these steps again. Following the almost waddling gait that made each step seem painful, my new friend continued to look back and smile and beckon me after her as if she were leading a reluctant child. I remembered how Miss Lettie had spoken boldly during the Civil Rights Movement and defended the protests of local black leaders. That had almost gotten her fired. Even earlier she'd asked black women to attend special gatherings when missionaries visited, and she arranged for the young people at our church to play the softball team at the African Methodist Episcopal church. Some people wanted to get rid of her even then, but it was not her work with the black community that undid her.

"Miss Lettie, you done got a visitor."

"Jack! How wonderful to see you!" She knew me before I'd even gotten through the door and whirled her wheelchair around to face me. The stroke that had crippled her limbs had not diminished the brightness of her face and cheerful clarity of her speech.

"You still remember me."

"I'll jus' leave y'all alone. Call me if'n you needs some'um."

"It's been over twenty years since I saw you. You were just a little boy, but I couldn't very well forget you, Jack." Her voice was as deep and resonant as always, and for the third time the heat rushed from my forehead down to my collar revealing chagrin and regret even deeper than my other recent embarrassments.

It hadn't been my intention to kneel beside her wheelchair nor to weep nor to speak in words choked with emotion. "Miss Lettie, I'm so sorry. I hate myself for what I did to you."

She tussled my hair as she'd done over two decades ago after I'd finished singing a solo with the junior choir. "Jack, Jack. You were just a boy. You didn't mean any harm. You didn't understand anything about what you thought you saw."

"You're wrong. I was proud. It was exciting to tell everyone about . . ." The words stuck in my throat as I sobbed, almost placing my head in Miss Lettie's lap.

"You always loved the story of Joseph in Egypt. It was your favorite as I recall. Don't you remember when Joseph said to his brothers down in Egypt, *Even though people may think evil of me, God meant it for good?* If I hadn't been moved away, I might never have met George Jones. He was a widower with a precious teenage girl and boy, and they became my children. Now I have three grandchildren—see their photographs here beside my bed!"

"How did you get through it? How did you survive such a terrible thing?"

"Oh, Jack, life goes on. Now tell me about yourself. Do you still sing? How wonderful that you became a priest. I always knew you would. How strange that you're now serving the church that Father Wardlaw served for so many years after we left your town—you see I've kept up with you through friends and church newsletters over the years. Did you ever see him again . . . after we left?"

"No, he died at the parish he served for so many years, where I'm the rector now, several years before I was called there. I never saw him after he left town . . . where I grew up and you . . . I'm so sorry." I told myself to stop weeping, stop that crying, as if I were hearing Miss Lettie's voice repeating the words.

"Father Wardlaw had just learned that my aunt had died, the aunt who reared me. I was weeping, as you are now; and he bent over and kissed me just as you came in the door. He meant nothing wrong by it. Heavens above, we were both over fifty years old! It was impulsive, foolish; but there was never anything romantic between us. Nothing at all. Still, we couldn't have explained it . . . or denied it; but it was all perfectly innocent."

"I know that now. I'm so very sorry."

"Here, Jack. Quit saying you're sorry, and for heaven's sake quit crying, and give me a kiss."

As I pecked her cheek, she turned her face up. "On the lips, if you please." And I felt the cells of my spirit coming alive and uniting together as the blood of my soul surged through its arteries and veins. "Thank you, Miss Lettie. Thank you."

"Just remember, life goes on. Whatever happens to you, life goes on."

# Blesséd Savior

"Please give Professor Penelope Sterling another round of applause to thank her for coming out here tonight." The applause was moderate, more than Penny might have expected. At least she heard no boos like the ones after her last couple of presentations. A few students clapped loudly. She could see others with folded hands and tightened, grim lips sitting in total silence. "Professor Sterling has agreed to answer a few questions. We have time for three or four. Please keep them short, and don't make speeches yourselves." Ben Harold grinned as he parroted Penny's last line of instruction to him. "Yes, Joe, in the third row." Ben pointed as the boy wearing a flannel shirt and bluejeans rose to speak. He looked like a farmer's son. Many of the students in this rural community college lived on nearby farms, although most of their parents had other jobs to supplement their agricultural income.

"Professor Sterling, how can you have laws and a moral code without believing that God revealed them?"

"That's an excellent question. We can derive laws and moral codes from our study of science and from the accumulated wisdom of human experience over the eras of human history. We don't need a deity to dictate them from heaven. As you may know, I ascribe such so-called revelations to either outright deception or, more charitably, to delusion." Penny wondered if she'd gone too far in her response.

"May I ask a follow-up question, Dr. Harold"?"

"Go ahead, Joe."

"How can you keep them from being just arbitrary, if they're not anchored in religious certainty?"

"By trial-and-error over centuries and centuries. That's part of the risk and responsibility of what it means to be human—that there are no easy answers, no neat and complete solutions."

"Thank you, ma'am."

Penny made a mental note to ask Ben about Joe. She would like to have a longer conversation with him if she should come back to visit the campus. He showed real potential and promise. The other questions were the typical washed-in-the-blood-of-Jesus, afraid-of-going-to-hell, what-the-Bible-says literalism that she heard after every reading from her book, *The Delusion of the God Myth*.

"You're a brave woman, Penny. I don't know how you can stand up and take all that hostility. You must have a streak of masochism in you." Ben smiled at her again with his infectious grin.

"I do it for kids like Joe. Maybe I can prod a few like him to think for themselves. Can you tell me more about him?"

"He's a bright boy. Maybe one of the few that may go on to the University if we can get some scholarship help for him."

"Could you arrange for me to talk with him if I come back here?"

"Absolutely. And I'm counting on a return visit. You want to get some coffee after I close up the place?

"Thanks anyway. I better head on home. I've got an early class tomorrow. Maybe another time?" Penny tried to convey a hopeful tone in her final question.

"Absolutely. I'll count on it."

Almost all the students had left the campus by the time that Penny reached the parking lot. Ben Harold was still inside securing the building. The large vapor lights must have been turned off after the scheduled night classes ended—another cost-saving measure necessitated by the cuts that the State Legislature had enacted for higher education. Only a few dim street lamps illuminated the darkened lot, like four hazy moons surrounding some distant planet. Penny shivered, even though the autumn nights were not yet chilly. She stumbled and almost fell on a piece of broken asphalt. She clicked the medallion on her key ring to unlock her car.

Then she heard the roar of the car racing toward her even before its headlights blinded her. As it screeched to a stop, the driver's door was flung open against her and knocked her to the ground, and she dropped her keys. She had raised herself on one knee with her other foot on the ground poised to stand up as the man snatched at her blouse and ripped it from her shoulders. Another man who had emerged from the passenger's side of the car grabbed her from behind and prevented her from fighting off her first assailant, a battle she had begun to win against someone who was actually smaller and weaker than she was. The man behind her began pulling down her skirt, but he never spoke. The little man in front of her had opened his fly and exposed his erect penis.

"I'll ram my rod in yer godless hell-hole pussy and fuck yer atheist brains plumb out'a yer skull, you damned blasphemous whore."

Penny became vaguely aware of an old pick-up truck slowly entering the perimeter of the parking lot and then moving more rapidly toward them with a knocking put-put sound. When the truck stopped near them, she thought she saw a large older black man approaching them.

"What you white boys doin'? You better leave out befo' you get in a heap o' trouble."

"Git out'a cher, nigger. 't ain't none a yer business."

"You let her a'loose." Out of the corner of her eye Penny could see the black man raise his arm with something in his hand, perhaps a tire iron.

"Jump in her car, Jimmy. Leastways we can git that much."

"You stay right there, Missy. I'uz gonna save you." As the robber who had held her from behind got into her car with her keys in his hand, the rapist got into his car whose motor was still running; and the black man ran toward his pick-up truck whose motor had also been left running. "Don't you worry 'bout nothin', Missy. I ain't about to let them hoodlums get away."

As the back wheel of her car threw up loose gravel and crossed her leg, Penny felt a blinding pain and passed out. Later she was told that the black man had driven his pick-up truck in front of the assailant's car causing it to crash head-on just as the police car arrived from the call that Ben Harold had made after he'd heard the commotion in the parking lot, never imagining that it involved Penny.

Before the policemen could get out of the patrol car the black man had scooped Penny into his arms and was carrying her toward his truck to take her to the hospital. Then the police had arrested the black man along with the assailant who had crashed his car.

Penny regained consciousness long enough to say, "No! No, he's not involved. He saved me."

BECAUSE HER LEG HAD been so badly crushed, Penny remained in the hospital almost four weeks for several orthopedic surgeries and rehabilitation. One bright outcome was Ben Harold's daily visits. He brought her flowers (or more often a single rose bud) or a humorous card and in his usual wry manner always had a comic quip to take her mind off feeling sorry for herself.

"You don't have to come every day, Ben. I know how busy you are." Penny wanted him to come every day but didn't want him to feel obligated.

"I feel guilty about what happened to you."

"It's not your fault. Surely you know that. After all, you teach logic." Penny hoped that he would continue to come because he wanted to see her, not because he felt guilty.

"I come every day because I want to see you, and now I have an excuse." Ben seemed to read her thoughts. "That's the first time I've seen you smile. Great!"

On her second day in the hospital Penny had remembered to ask Ben about the black man who had rescued her. She wanted to learn his name so that she could thank him, reimburse him for the damage to his truck, in some way reward him. Ben thought that perhaps the police had written down his name; and when he called the police station, Ben learned that the black man was still in jail because the authorities believed he'd been involved in the plot to rob Penny. She was distraught that his heroic act resulted in his punishment and suffering. She relied on Ben to convey to the police the true story of his bravery in defending her, and she was relieved to learn that he was released immediately.

Not until her second week in the hospital did Penny overcome her reluctance to make any further requests of Ben and ask him to track the black man down and inquire if he could visit her in the hospital so that she could offer some recompense. She felt awkward continuing to ask Ben for favors, but his willing eagerness to help her seemed to bring them closer.

On her second Friday in the hospital Penny was roused from dozing by a gentle knock on her door.

"Come in."

The black man entered the room cautiously like an animal surveying a strange place. Penny had learned that his name was William Moody. He was holding a bouquet of garden mums and asters with their stems wrapped in a newspaper cone.

"I see you done got lots of purty store-bought flowers. I jus' brung you a few poseys out 'a Lily's garden."

"They're beautiful. You shouldn't have. You've already done so much for me. How kind of you to visit me, Mr. Moody."

"They ain't much." He looked around seeking a place to lay them down.

"Do you mind emptying that vase of wilted roses? Just dump them in the trashcan and put some fresh water in the vase for your flowers. They're lovely."

"You shore you wants to throw out them store-bought roses for these here garden blossoms?"

"Please, please, Mr. Moody. I cherish them. Your wife grew them herself?"

"Yes 'um. But you can jus' call me Willie."

"If you call me Penny. My name is Penelope, but my friends call me Penny."

"My family call me William, but mos' folks, white folks I works for, calls me Willie."

"I'd like to call you William, if you don't mind. I feel as though we're special friends after all you did for me."

"That'ud be fine by me." William smiled, and Penny saw a gold tooth on one side of his mouth and a broken tooth on the other side. His hair was salted with gray, and his face was strong and ageless, like a warrior's; but his arms were muscled and youthful, like an athlete's. "Wadn't a whole big thing."

"Of course it was. You may have saved my life, certainly saved me . . ." Penny glanced away and shivered.

William spoke quickly, softly, as if to cover her embarrassment. "I hear tell you be a doctor."

"Not a medical doctor." Penny thought he would assume any doctor was a physician. "I'm a teacher."

"I knows that. Over at the University."

"That's right." Penny decided it was time to come to the point. "I want to reimburse you and give you some kind of reward, too. You missed several days of work on my account when the police arrested you by mistake, and your truck was damaged when you used it . . . to . . . ." She realized that she was grasping for words even as the illiterate black man spoke easily.

"Not much account that ol' truck, so beat up I don't hardly bother fixin' it no more, long as it'll run. I jus' takes a hammer and beats out the dents and keeps on a goin'." He laughed easily, freely; and Penny laughed with him. He seemed to put her at ease, rather than vice versa.

"Still, I want to give you a reward. At least a few hundred dollars."

"I couldn't take no money, Miss Penny. I truly believes God sent me to take care a' you. I really believes that. Seein' you gettin' back you' strength, that be reward enough for me. I couldn't take nothin' else."

"But I want to give you something, do something for you."

"What you teach over at the University, Miss Penny?"

"Just call me Penny, plain Penny, please. I teach philosophy and ethics." Penny wondered if he would be able to understand anything about what those words referred to.

"Ethics tell all about how folks ought to behave. That right?"

"That's exactly right."

"I hear tell you done wrote a famous book. Do it be all about ethics?"

"Yes. In part."

"I jus' be a ignorant black man, Miss . . . I never got pas' the seventh grade, . . . Penny; but I'd love to read you' book, if'n you feel like you have to give me some'um."

"I don't believe in God, William. I'm what you call an atheist. That's part of the book, too."

"I done heerd about all that. I pro'bly won't understand all what you say, but I'd still love to read you' book, best as I can. That the only reward I be willin' to take off a' you, if'n you let me."

"I'll have my friend take a copy around to your house."

"No call for that. I be visitin' you ever' day or so, if'n you don't mind, and I can pick it up here at the hospital. I got to see how you be gettin' on."

"I'd love for you to visit, but I don't want to cause you any more trouble . . . but if you're in the area, I'd really like to see you." Penny meant every word she spoke, and William visited her regularly for the next two weeks. She looked forward to his visits almost as much as she anticipated Ben's visits. In all truth she sometimes enjoyed the time she spent with William even more than her visits with Ben.

WILLIAM VISITED PENNY AT least every other day, and Ben visited every day. Penny found Ben's visits entertaining and William's visits comforting. William often noticed when Penny had slumped into the bed. "Look a'here, Penny, let me prop you up some and fluff out your pillas."

William's smile and sheer presence relaxed Penny; she could feel the muscles in her back and shoulders loosen as soon as he came into the room. He filled her pitcher with fresh water and ice. He tidied her nightstand. He held his strong arm behind her and adjusted the straw to her lips. He opened the Venetian blinds to let some afternoon sunlight into the room. He raised or lowered the bed to its most comfortable position, often without even asking her before he did it but always saying afterward, "Does that feel 'bout right, Penny? You let me know how you likes it." And without any prevarication she always replied, "That's just right. So much better."

One afternoon during her third week in the hospital Penny expressed her concern. "I worry about all the time you spend with me, William. It takes you away from your work." She'd learned that he earned his living as a handy man who did odd jobs and repairs. Ben had told her that he'd heard that William could fix about anything.

"Don't you worry none 'bout that. God done sent me to take care a' you."

"You know I don't believe in God, William."

"I done heerd that from you afore. Besides which I done read your book."

"Did you like it?" Penny ventured cautiously, knowing that both she and William knew she'd meant, "Did you understand it?"

"I just be a ignorant, uneducated ol' black man, as well you know; but I follow the gist a' it. I follow you' reasoning right good. Couldn't find no fault with it. Course I had to read it with the dictionary on one knee and it on t'other." He grinned, and they both laughed. They both seemed to laugh a lot when they were together.

"It didn't make you wonder a little whether God exists?" Penny was even comfortable teasing him now.

"No ma'am. God done tol' me to take care a' you, like I said befo'." William could tease Penny and give her back as good as she gave. Perhaps that was why she felt comfortable talking with him.

"Do you actually hear words in your head when God talks to you?"

"Lawd 'a mercy, no. It more like when Lily be cookin' supper and hummin' to herself and look over at me and smile, and we knows what each other be thinkin' whole lots better than when she be blabberin' away. Some'um like that. Not the same, a'course."

"You're a wise man, William."

"No ways. But I reads. I reads most all the time. Whenever I quit school 'cause my family need the money, I start inta readin' books. Most ever' night I be readin'. I never cared for the television all that much. Ever' night I reads me a book, like you's. Some I agrees with. Some not so much, but I learns from all of 'em, mos' 'specially them what I disagrees with, like you's." William smiled. They both laughed.

Penny found it easier to talk with William about religion than anyone else she'd ever known. He didn't try to argue with her and use spurious logic like other fundamentalists. He didn't try to impress her with obsequious flattery. He didn't try to identify himself with her by embracing her ideas, like Ben. Above all, he didn't condemn her like her father who had cursed her with his dying breath because of her beliefs. In fact, William began to feel like a surrogate father to Penny and seemed to accept her for who she was, as she was.

"How is it you've never told me how wrong I am, not to believe in God?"

"What all somebody believes is they own business. Ain't no way a man should go an' tell somebody else what all to believe."

"But you believe in God. It's important to you."

"Penny, I needs all the help I can get. I ain't smart and educated like you. Maybe you don't need God all the ways I do."

Only once during her month of confinement in the hospital did Ben and William visit Penny at the same time. William came first, and as soon as Ben entered the room William rose to leave. "I reckon I better get out a' chere, so as you can talk to your boyfriend." William smiled, but no one laughed this time. It was as if his words had enacted some paternal edict that brought a new reality into being. It also seemed to break open the separate silent longings in Penny and Ben, and they began to talk with each other about their relationship and to express their love for one another and to explore the possibility of a future together.

THREE DAYS BEFORE PENNY was scheduled to be discharged from the hospital, Ben proposed having a celebration for her at his apartment. Penny had hoped that he might propose with an engagement ring rather than planning a party for her. In spite of all her unconventional ideas about religion and society, she still yearned for a traditional marriage.

"I'm not sure I'm up to a party, Ben. I appreciate your thought, but . . ."

"We're beginning to get serious. I think we are . . . I know I'm not in your class intellectually, academically. I know my friends from the community college are kind of second-class brains compared to your colleagues at the University, but I thought it might be a chance to see if our friends and colleagues could get along, and if we had something in common . . ."

"I never thought about it like that . . . Sure. Let's do it. Thank you. It's a wonderful idea."

"Maybe we could bill it as your resurrection party. It's not as clever as your puns on religion, but . . ."

"It's great. Just my kind of humorous blasphemy!"

"Who'd you like to invite?"

"My colleagues in the department, of course. I'll give you the names of two or thee others from the University. And, oh yes, William Moody."

"The black man? Don't you think he'd be a little out of his element, over his head? Why?"

"I want to be able to give him some public recognition for what he did for me. And, oh, don't call it a resurrection party when you ask him."

"Why on earth not? I've never known you to spare a jab at a fundamen-talist, regardless of who is was and how they felt. You've made a career out of it. A very successful career, I might add."

When Penny talked with William the next day about the party, she learned that Ben had already called to invite him.

"Me and Lily'll be comin'. But jus' to tell you, I won't be drinkin' no liquor. I done been down that road, and I ain't a'goin' back. I done had more 'an my share 'a the hard stuff and fast livin'."

Penny assured him that there would be alternative beverages.

THE RESURRECTION PARTY WAS a great success. All of Penny's and Ben's friends were so charmed by the idea of their romantic involvement that those from the University didn't flaunt their superior status and those from the community college didn't fawn like dogs with tails tucked between their legs. Penny reigned over the gathering like a queen on her throne, with her leg in a cast hiked onto the coffee table supported by pillows. She need not have worried about William. He was the hit of the evening as the guests began to solicit his suggestions for raising tomatoes and repairing dry wall and fixing leaky faucets. He became the savant amidst the sages; and his wife, Lily, held her own in the exchange of opinions between the academics.

William visited less frequently at Penny's home than his every other day drop-ins had been at the hospital. He stopped by almost every week, never missing more than two weeks. He always brought her something—a slice of his sugar cured ham or some Brunswick stew and even a little plaque of an owl he'd carved "for the smart lady."

Penny wracked her brain about what to give William in return and finally hit on books. Each time he visited, she had a book waiting to present to him. William seemed to be delighted with their exchanges, and the books gave them something to talk about, although they never lacked for easy conversation even before he began reading the books that Penny gave him.

"You know how much I enjoy your visits, William; but I hate to take up so much of your time."

"God done tol' me to take care a' you, as you well knows. Whether you believes it or not is another thing. And some'um always need fixin' at this ol' house."

"Which reminds me—the light's flickering in my study."

"Bad connection. I get right to it fo' you."

Although Penny insisted on paying William for his work, she suspected that he didn't charge her his usual fees. "William, I believe you can do just about anything."

"Near 'bouts, 'ceptin' people problems. Speakin' a' which, how you and Mista Ben gettin' 'long together? You gonna jump the broom?" William turned over his palms toward the ceiling and paused to see if Penny could understand his lingo as well as he understood hers.

"He hasn't asked me. I think he feels unworthy. He didn't get his PhD from as prestigious a school as I did, and he's never published." Penny would not have said these things to anyone except William, as if he were the father to whom she could confide everything, the father she never had.

"You care about all them things, Penny?"

"Not a whit of it."

"Then you gotta let him know. Lily she finished high school and went on to college. I knows. I'uz feelin' jus' like Mista Ben, but Lily she let me see I had jus' as much as her . . ." William tapped his temple. ". . . in my thick head, just as good."

That night Penny found the right words to reassure Ben, and the following week he proposed and presented her with an engagement ring.

As THE DATE FOR the trial of Penny's assailants drew closer, she became more and more nervous about encountering them. Nightmares afflicted her when she was able to sleep at all, and several times each day she became agitated and had difficulty breathing. At just such a moment of panic the doorbell rang; but when she peered out the window of her living room, she was relieved to see William standing on her porch holding a split oak basket with something leafy lapping over its top rim.

"You has any likin' for turnips and greens, Penny?"

"I love them. I grew up craving them."

William laughed so hard he had to set the basket down and hold his side. "I done figured you for a country gal."

For the first time in days Penny laughed, too. "William, I have a favor to ask you. A big favor."

"Ain't that a wonder! You ain't never axed me a favor befo'e. Ain't never axed me for nothin', 'ceptin' doin' a few chores to fix up yo' house."

"I know you'll have to testify at the trial. You're the only one who saw the face of the man who held me from behind. Even though the police identified him when they picked him up in my car later that night, you're the only one who saw him in the parking lot." Penny felt short of breath again and a rising fluttering panic in her chest. She sighed. "But, William, would you be willing to stay with me for the rest of the trial? I know it would take you away from your work. I'd be glad to reimburse you for . . ."

"Penny, Penny, Penny. Hush up. You think I'd go and do anythin' different from stayin' right by you?"

Penny had the impulse to hug William, but she restrained herself and wiped her sweaty palms on her skirt. "In graduate school they said I was tough, mean and cold. They called me Pure Copper. I hated it, but now I wish I were that strong and hard." She was about to explain the pun on her name to William, but as usual he was one step ahead of her.

"Like Sterlin', Pure; an' Penny, Copper. Jus' plain Penny, like you tol' me befo'. That's a good 'un." William slapped his side and laughed again and then began grappling in the pocket of his overalls. He brought out a penny that exactly matched his skin and laid it across his forearm. "Looks to me like a right good color. Leastways we done got some'um we shares. You be tough and strong, if you needs to, jus' like me; but ain't neither one a' us hard and cold. No ways."

"Thank you, William. It means more to me than . . ."

"Mista Ben gonna be there at the trial with you?"

"I don't know. I hope so. He's got classes, and . . ."

"I reckon he gonna be right there with us."

WILLIAM SAT ON ONE side of Penny and Ben on her other side throughout the trial. The defense lawyer thought he could shake the testimony of an ignorant black man and be awarded a lesser sentence than the district at-torney had offered for a guilty plea, but William was articulate and detailed in his own ungrammatical way and unshaken by cross-examination.

Penny could remember very little from the trial after it was over, as if its pain and torment became blotted out of her memory like the events of the attack itself, except for her pride in William's words and his strong, calm, unshakable manner and her comfort as Ben held her hand hour after hour, never releasing his firm, gentle grasp. With her surrogate father and her future husband on each side of her, she felt safer and more secure than she'd ever been in her life. The culprits both received sentences of twenty-five to forty years in prison, and the district attorney assured Penny that even with the very best behavior they would serve at least fifteen years.

As Penny and William and Ben came out of the courthouse, Ben rushed away to teach an afternoon class. William asked Penny if she would like for him to follow her home. "No thanks. That's kind and thoughtful, but I'm fine. You've done enough. It's over now."

Penny watched William's pick-up truck driving slowly away and noticed the dents that had been made in it when he'd blocked the thief, dents that he intentionally left, like the dents in her psyche that would never go away however much she healed.

Then she saw Joe approaching her. It was ironic that Penny had often thought about Joe and his questions and had imagined a dialogue with him during the past couple of weeks as she was writing an article for a profes-sional journal that she'd titled, "Ethics in the Age of Post-Monotheism."

"Congratulations, Professor Sterling. I'm glad those bastards got a lot of years behind bars. Pardon my language."

"Why, hello, Joe. Did you attend the trial?"

"Yes, ma'am. You remembered my name! I wanted to see how it all came out. We were real sorry about what happened to you, us students. You didn't deserve anything like that."

"Thank you, Joe. I appreciate all the cards you students sent me in the hospital. They meant a lot."

"You got a minute, Professor Sterling? I wanted to ask you something."

"Sure."

"I read your book. Some parts I read two or three times. Dr. Harold he's got it all arranged for me to go to the University next year. I was thinking about majoring in philosophy. I really like the way you reason things out. But I was wondering if I can still believe in God and take philosophy."

"You'll be graded on your arguments and your ability to reason, Joe, not on your beliefs."

"But if I took your classes, would it make any difference if I still believe in God?"

"It might make a tremendous difference, but it wouldn't necessarily work to your detriment." Penny reflected how different her responses to Joe were than they would have been before she'd met William, how then they would probably have been clever and snide and demeaning of organized religion. It was not that she herself believed anything different, she thought, it was just that since she'd met William she responded differently to people.

"Thank you, ma'am. Thank you so much! I really do want to learn more about philosophy."

"I'm glad."

"Bye now." He turned and moved several steps away.

"And Joe . . ."

"Yes ma'am?"

". . . let me know if I can help you. Stop by my office, and I'll do whatever I can for you."

"Yes ma'am! Yes ma'am! Absolutely! You can count on it." Penny heard Ben's words and inflections imitated by his student. "Thank you so, so much. I will. You can count on it!"

PENNY HAD PROGRESSED FROM a heavy plaster cast to a hard fiberglass cast to a walking cast that she could unstrap and remove from her leg to sleep at night, but she had not felt well for several weeks. A pain sometimes shot through her leg that ached more than it had since she was in the hospital.

Although Penny didn't remember what happened the night the pain had become almost unbearable, she was told later how she was found after she'd lost consciousness sometime during the night. William had come to bring her some vegetables. When there was no response to his knock, he'd looked through the living room window and seen her unconscious on the floor.

As he broke the window a neighbor had called the police to report, "A black peeping Tom's looking in Miss Sterling's window. They Lord God! He's breaking into her house. Get here quick!"

William had reached the hospital and carried Penny into the emergency room by the time the police caught up with him. He'd explained what had happened, and this time they believed him. "It's *déjà vu* all over again," one of the policemen had said. "Willie Moody, how many times we gotta go through this all over again with you?"

By the time that Ben arrived the doctor told them that William had gotten Penny to the hospital in the nick of time. "Another hour and she would have been dead for sure." The doctor was able to dissolve the clot that had migrated from her injured leg to her lung and relieve the pulmonary embolism before it did any mortal damage.

The next day Penny was still somewhat groggy from the anesthesia when she woke from a nap and saw William standing beside her bed. "William, you're my blessèd savior. You saved me. You saved my life for a second time."

"I done tol' you, Penny. God sent me to take care a' you, whatever you thinks, and I gonna take care a' you best ways I can, long as I can. I gone over yest'day evenin' and nail a board crost you' window that I busted out. If you tell Mista Ben to meet up and let me inside, I fix it proper."

"Ben can give you a key, but he doesn't have to let you in. Just keep the key until I get home. After all, you're like family. I'll pay you . . ."

"You ain't payin' me nothin'. I done busted out the window, and I gonna fix it." William grinned. "That my gift to you, free and clear."

PENNY HAD BEEN HOME from her second hospitalization almost a month and was puzzled that she hadn't seen William for over two weeks when she heard a familiar tapping on her front door. "William," she thought with strangely thrilled excitement; but when she opened the door she saw William's wife, Lily, carrying his split oak basket filled with vegetables.

"William made me promise to get these vegetables around to you."

"Where is he? Is he all right?"

"He's in the hospital. He had a heart attack. It's right bad."

"When can I see him?"

"Whenever you're able. This afternoon if you feel up to it. There are limited visiting hours at the cardiac intensive care unit where they have him."

Penny met Lily in the hospital lobby, which was all too familiar, and caused her to shiver slightly as they walked toward the elevator. When they approached the desk to register in the cardiac intensive care waiting room, a stern receptionist peered over her half-frame spectacles and growled in a husky voice as she scowled at the tall, dirty-blonde, blue-eyed, pale-skinned Penny standing beside the small, wiry black woman, "Only family members can go inside."

Lily opened her eyes wide and radiated a searing look at the receptionist that could have melted Medusa, and with great authority responded, "She *is* family."

The receptionist withered and began to look like the drooping flowers in the vase on her desk. "Sign here. It'll be about fifteen minutes. The doctors are running behind with their rounds."

After they sat down Penny glanced at Lily, not sure she could say what she was thinking as she faced the stern countenance; but now Lily's face had softened and reflected a kindness and gentleness even deeper than William's. "I know white people say all the time that black people who help them are *like family* . . ." Penny choked, and her voice became frail, like a scared little girl's. "But when I told William he was like family, I really, truly meant it. William's like a father . . ." She wanted to tell Lily about her life-long conflicts over religion with her father and how William had become a surrogate father to her, but she couldn't yet form the words.

"I know, honey. William feels the same way. Our children are on the way here, one from Chicago and one from Phoenix. Of course, they love him. He was a good father, a loving father, when he was around; but he was in jail so much of the time—in the state penitentiary for a while—as they were growing up . . . Even when he was at home, he was drunk or strung out on drugs so much . . . It's so different now. He feels like you're a second chance for him. He really feels like God gave him another child when you were dropped into his life."

"How is he?" Penny paused and choked again. "Will he make it?"

"It's touch and go, but the doctors are very hopeful. You should be aware before we go in there that he comes in and out of consciousness. One minute he's clear as a bell and the next he's out of it or sound asleep from the medications."

The double doors flung open with a thud, and the family members moved slowly but steadily toward the interior hall of the cardiac unit, overcome by a mixture of fear and hope. Lily guided Penny and pulled aside the curtain of William's cubical.

"Penny! You done come an' see me!"

"I would've come sooner, if I'd known . . ."

"Wouldn't've done no good. I warn't in my right mind till yest'day."

"Oh, William, I do love you." Penny took his hand and glanced up to see if Lily approved, and Lily smiled at her.

"That do me a world a' good."

"You saved my life. Twice. If I could just . . ."

"You be savin' my life right now. I saves your life, and you saves my life. That what we do in this here world, savin' one another, followin' the steps a' Jesus, best ways we can, whether we owns up to it or not." William laughed and choked.

"You're talking too much, William. Slow down some." Lily looked over at Penny. "That's the first time he's laughed since he came into the hospital. It's a good sign."

"Say some'um'll make me feel better, Penny. Say some'um'll get me all well."

Penny could think of no words to say. Her mind seemed to have been emptied like a bottle of milk dropped on the floor that was spilling out its contents. Then the words came into her mind from long ago. They seemed to be the only words left in her mind. "Our Father, who art in heaven, hallowed be thy name. Thy kingdom come, thy will be done, on earth as it is in heaven."

Even as Penny spoke she thought, "I don't believe a word of this." It was as if someone else were speaking the words through her.

"Give us this day our daily bread, and forgive us our debts as we forgive our debtors."

William began speaking in unison with Penny "And lead us not into temptation, but deliver us from evil."

William's eyes closed; and even though Penny heard him snoring softly, she continued speaking. "For thine is the kingdom and the power and the glory forever and ever. Amen."

William's eyes opened, and he grinned. "A-men!" Then he winked at Penny, and Lily laughed.

# *Acknowledgments*

My thanks are extended to many people who assisted in the publication of this book.

Richard Mills immediately agreed to contribute the painting for the cover. Rick was a member of two parishes that I served: St. Wilfrid's Episcopal Church in Marion, Alabama, when he taught art at Judson College and where we shared some of the experiences and knew some of the people who evoked these stories, and Grace Episcopal Church in Mt. Meigs, Alabama, when he taught art at Auburn University Montgomery.

Joel Sanders edited these stories with a clear and careful eye for details and inconsistencies. Short passages were rewritten, some several times, under his expert guidance. However it is appraised, the book was much improved by his suggestions.

None of my three books would have been published without the encouragement and judicious generosity of Randall Williams and the staff of NewSouth Books.

Finally, my wife, Rilla, proofread these stories through so many revisions that she might be able to recite them from memory. Any errors that may still exist probably occur from my later inveterate revising of the text.

www.ingramcontent.com/pod-product-compliance
Lightning Source LLC
Chambersburg PA
CBHW031310280626
47169CB00017B/1178